F   Parris, P. B.
Par
     Waltzing in the attic

DATE DUE

No 3 '90			
No 16 '90	NY 27 '94	AUG 3 1 2001	DE 3 1 200
Ja 12 '9	JUL 1 6 1996		
Ja 15 '91	AUG 3 0 1996	OCT 1 5 2001	
Ja 29 '91			
Fe 27 '91	DEC 3 1 1997		
AUG 25 '92	NO 16 '98		
	OC 15 '99		
JA 14 '9			
NOV 2 2	DE 16 2000		
DEC 6 1998	APR 2 5 200		

Waltzing
in the
Attic

P. B. Parris

DOUBLEDAY
NEW YORK LONDON TORONTO SYDNEY AUCKLAND

PUBLISHED BY DOUBLEDAY

a division of Bantam Doubleday Dell Publishing Group, Inc.
666 Fifth Avenue, New York, New York 10103

DOUBLEDAY and the portrayal of an anchor
with a dolphin are trademarks of Doubleday,
a division of Bantam Doubleday Dell
Publishing Group, Inc.

Portions of the novel appeared, in a slightly different form, in
The Albany Review and *The MacGuffin.*

Library of Congress Cataloging-in-Publication Data
Parris, P. B.
Waltzing in the attic / P. B. Parris. —1st ed. in the U.S.A.
p.   cm.
I. Title.
PS3566.A754W3   1990
813'.54—dc20   89-25911
                                                                        CIP
ISBN 0-385-41272-X

Printed in the United States of America
August 1990
FIRST EDITION
BVG

My thanks to Ellyn Bache, Margaret-Love Denman, Charlotte Maxwell, Geraldine Powell, and Elizabeth Squire. And my most sincere gratitude to Nan A. Talese for her insight and sensitivity.

For
my sons
Christopher, Andrew,
Timothy, and Patrick

The men called it God's country—
but the women asked, who else wants it?
—Wright Morris

Waltzing
in the
Attic

Chapter 1

1987

I can stand just as still as he can, for just as long as he can. I can outwait anybody.

The banty rooster tilts his head and looks at me like he knows my mind. "Listen to me, you old fornicator," I say. "It's your time." I crouch down. I take a slow step forwards, careful not to catch the bottom of my apron. I stretch my arms out, ready to grab him by the neck. His black tail feathers flash green in the light through the henhouse door. His red wattles, like swollen privates, quiver. I run towards him and grab—but all I catch is his shadow. He dashes into a huddle of hens, and they scatter and flap, raising dust and a racket like a tin can full of rusty nails.

Alone now in the far corner, he poses like a picture in a hatchery catalog, staring at me. "You stringy old cock, you're not good for a thing," I say. "I don't even want to fool with you, you're so worthless." I haven't been chasing

1

chickens for most of my seventy years without figuring out how to put them off guard.

The hens keep on clucking and fluttering and upsetting each other back behind me. The rooster and me, neither one blinks. "You mean old sinner," I say, real slow. A sudden squawk sends the hens scattering, making the rooster look away. I fly towards him, my hands closing around his neck, but he pulls his head down into himself and slips away, skittering across to the row of nest boxes nailed to the wall. I land flat on my belly, and he struts, and it sounds like he laughs under his hateful breath.

It knocked the wind out of me when I fell and slid forwards, knees dug deep into feathers and filth. My left forearm's bruised, and it hurts. I scramble up, panting, and brush the dried chicken droppings off my apron and housedress. I don't give up easy. I'm going to have this old reprobate, one way or the other. Rubbing the loose, freckled, old-lady skin on my arm, I work the ache out with my fingers. I take my stand again in front of where he's scratching at some straw that's fell out of the nests. I wait.

The hens quiet down, and he stops looking back at me. He moves the straw with his feet and pecks at the dirt. He's found something, a bug maybe, and while he's busy trying to catch it, I step forwards and grab him around the middle. I squeeze his wings down tight. He kicks his feet and tries to scratch me. I hold him away with my elbows bent out to make a circle. "Now I got you, you old devil."

Jabbering and complaining, the flock scatters when I carry him out through the chicken yard. I take that mean old bird by the feet and hold him upside down while I go out the gate and fasten the hasp with a piece of twisted wire, all rusted and hard for old fingers to work one-handed. I've always kept my chickens in a fenced yard, like Mutti before me. I never let them run wild and scavenge like orphans.

"Silly, silly girls," I say back at the flock of white and orange and black-and-white hens, "you're better off without that old lecher to bother you, believe me."

He swings from my hand, his neck bent so he can look up at me like he thinks he can make me leave go with those wicked yellow eyes.

The axe stands up stiff, its sharp face buried in the tree stump we use for a chopping block. I run my free hand along its smooth handle, warm in the afternoon sun. Looking across the barnyard and down the drive next to the house, I can see across the county road to the cornfields that used to be ours, Vater's and then Karl's. For want of rain, the stalks have dried and paled to a wore-out dun gray. The least little breeze sets the stiff leaves rustling, like the whisper of old gossips. And on a hot day like this is, it can fool you into thinking you hear running water.

Overhead, a crow flaps through the empty sky and caws, caws. I turn and follow it flying back over where half the wood shingles are gone off the barn roof and the rest have gone the color of ashes. Chinks of sky show through here and there like patches of fresh blue paint. The barn was red when I was a girl, though it's hard to see that these days. It had white trim too, I think.

Another crow caws and rises up to join the first one, and they talk back and forth over the top of the barn and out of sight. Far back as I can remember, I've always been a little mad at God cause I can't fly. I don't mean in an airplane or like that. I mean like a bird or an angel. I can understand how He made us all a little less than the angels, but a bird's just a dumb animal with a brain the size of a pea.

I can be mad at God. He doesn't punish you for that, at least not right away. Some folks He doesn't punish at all that He should. Sometimes you got to help Him along.

The rooster thrashes and turns in the hand down at my side. I shouldn't have looked up and let those crows distract me. He squawks and twists free, clawing my wrist, and shoots across the dusty, rutted barnyard and into the tall weeds where hollyhocks used to grow behind the house. "Now look what you done," I holler at him. "You old heathen, you've drawn blood." I plow in after him. I can see the stalks wavering where he runs ahead of me, but the growth is so thick I can't move fast as he can.

I lose sight of him in the weeds. I stop and shade my eyes with my hand, trying to make out where that old rascal's got to. Dear Lord, I'm hot. Sweat's running off my eyebrows and down my cheeks. The hair's pulling out of the knot at the back of my neck and falling forwards against my face. I hear the locust sawing in the windbreak behind me.

I don't see a thing moving in the weeds, so I walk over out of the heat into the shadow next to the house. The paint on the clapboards has weathered away, just like on the barn. At least none of the glass back here is broke. Not like around the front, where some of the windows have been out for fifty years and more.

From around the side of the house comes the puny crowing of that miserable rooster. I peek past the corner and spot him perched on the pile of bricks where the double chimney fell away from the house in the tornado years back. He puffs out his chest, feathers shiny black, and looks pleased with himself, but I'm not about to give up and let him persist in his evil ways.

As I commence climbing up one side of the tumbled bricks, he darts down the other side and off into the thick weeds, but now he's headed towards the old fence across the front yard. Step by step, I work him into the corner where Mutti's orange daylilies have gone wild. He raises up on his claws and flaps his wings, but he's trapped. "Now I got you," I say and grab him around the middle, tight. "This time," I say, "I'm not taking any chances." I lift him over my head and swing him around and around by his neck—"Die, you old sinner, die for your sins," I say —till he goes limp.

At the back door, Karl's feisty yellow dog, Little David, growls and moves like he wants to snatch the banty for his supper, but I hold it up out of his reach and go in and slam the door. Karl named him Little David cause he says the runty pup isn't scared of a thing. "No matter how big, not even a giant like Goliath vould he be scared of," Karl says. Too dumb to be scared, I say.

I pump a bucket of water at the sink, and my arm's hurting again. Devilish old bird, tricking me like that. With both hands, I heave the bucket over to the cast-iron cookstove to heat. I'm stoking up the fire with cobs when Karl comes into the kitchen, a stringy old man dressed like a scarecrow in overalls I've mended for years, patch on patch. He wears an oily brown felt hat indoors and out, winter and summer. I wonder sometimes if he even takes it off when he goes to bed. His glasses ride low on his nose, and his beard is bushy and dirty white. Stove up like that with what he calls "roomatiz," he shuffles along three-legged on Vater's black walnut cane *his* father brought over from the Old Country. Karl's seventy-six, many years older than Vater was when he died. Maybe it'll soon be time for Karl to go too.

"Hannah," he growls at me, "Gerta's calling you." Karl always sounds angry, just the way our father used to. Fact is, Karl looks just like him, bristly, with eyes like slivers of glass. He talks like Vater too, his *w*'s coming out like *v*'s. "Don't just stand there, girl. See vot she vants." Karl's got a black heart, and he likes bossing folks around. His sin is pride. And lechery.

I wipe my hands on my apron and go on through the dim front hall. In her room, Gerta slouches in her wheelchair. She's reading the Bible with a magnifying glass by the light of a kerosene lamp that's almost gone out. "It keeps flickering," she complains and puts the little red ribbon bookmark between the pages before she shuts it up.

Gerta's a year younger than our brother, Karl. Underneath the rouge, her color's bad, pasty. She never goes outdoors and always keeps the roller shades at the windows pulled clear down. Her white hair's thin, you can see pink scalp right through it. And she's got soft and fat from laying in bed all these years or sitting in a wheelchair and making me push her around the house though she can do it herself when she wants to.

Gerta was real stuck on herself and her looks once, and had a beau, a fiancé. Before the automobile accident, her sin was vanity. Now it's gluttony.

"The darn thing just needs some kerosene," I tell her, pointing at the lamp.

"Well, fix it then so I don't have to ruin my eyes. You

want to make me blind? Isn't crippled enough? Is that what you want?"

I figured out long ago there's no use arguing with Gerta, so I lean across to pick up the lamp. I can smell the sweet, flowery dusting powder Frederick buys her at the drugstore in town.

"Where're you going with that?" Gerta reaches up and grabs my arm. She's got strong hands from working the wheels of her chair. "You don't expect me to sit here in the dark, do you?"

"It's still light outdoors. Let me put up the shades for you while I refill the lamp." I take a step towards the windows, but she grips my arm even tighter.

"No, Hannah, no." I knew she'd get upset, that's why I said it. She hates the daylight. "Go get me another lamp, one with a full well. Then you can take this one away." She pinches my arm before leaving go. "And don't you go fooling with those window shades."

I'm coming back through the hall when my Pauli opens the back door and lets Little David in with him. "Get that dog out of my kitchen," I holler at him. "How many times do I have to tell you? Not till after we eat." Pauli's a grown man, thirty years old, but some of the time he acts like he's still a youngster, like he doesn't think what he's doing. He wrestles the yippy yellow dog back out the door while I get another lamp down from the pantry and fill it from the five-gallon can of kerosene under the sink. When I turn around to ask him to take it to Gerta, he's gone. That's about how much help I get from anybody around here. Pauli's sin is sloth. And lechery too.

He's gone into the back parlor with Karl. I can hear them in there, talking about watching the television again

tonight at Frederick's, most likely. Ever since Frederick
moved into that trailer house over by the windbreak, the
men spend most evenings there, leaving me up at the
house to keep Gerta company. At first, I didn't much care
—Gerta's been my cross for years—but when Frederick
bought that television and now something called a VCR
and never even asked me over for a look, I got sore. His sin
is greed and gluttony and lechery and every bless-ed mean
and hateful thing he can think up.

Some evenings after dark, I walk down and watch
through the trailer window. I can see all right. It's a little
hard to hear though. Sometimes if I get close enough to
catch the television sound, Little David, that's been laying
next to Karl's chair, commences whining and pawing to
get out. Then I have to hightail it back up to the house
before Karl lets the dog loose to scare away what he thinks
is maybe some trespassing stranger prowling around outside.

Last night when I got down there, I saw a naked lady
on the television. My face turned hot and my eyes got
watery. I never saw anybody showing off their nakedness
like that before. And those three wicked men were sitting
there, watching. I ran all the way back up to the house in
the dark, truly mortified. I couldn't hardly sleep the whole
night for the righteous anger building up in me.

"Hannah," Gerta yells. I go trade lamps in her room
and half listen to her grumblings about something or
other. Finally, she says she wants me to brush her hair. But
I got to tend to supper. My mind's on what I'm going to do
with that banty laying out there in the kitchen sink. "Get
me a glass of water," she yells at my back when I go out
the door. I pretend like I don't hear.

By now the bucket on the stove's boiling, so I dunk the old bird in long enough to scald him good and then yank his feathers off by the handfuls, tossing them into the sink. When he's stripped naked, looking sort of starved and sickly, I take my butcher knife and cut into him. I pull out the liver and the lights, the heart and the rope of intestines. I dump the offal in the sink. I know Little David would gobble it up if I was to chuck it all out to him, but I got other plans. The wages of sin is death. The food of sinners is chicken shit.

The bucket of water I used for scalding is still steaming on the stove. I chop up the intestines and cut the bowels into bite-size pieces and drop them into the boiling water. While that simmers, making broth, I cut up the stringy rooster and flour the pieces. I watch him sizzle and fry, like a sinner in Hell, in hot lard in the cast-iron skillet while I poke at him with Mutti's three-tine fork. I plan to boil some flour dumplings in the broth. Frederick will come home from the broom factory, and when those vain and lecherous folks come to the supper table, they'll fold their hands and bow their heads and blaspheme their prayers. They'll complain about the tough chicken and slurp down the broth and never wonder why I don't eat any.

If I was one of those black crows, I'd climb up the blue sky, up over the ruined house, and look down on the barn's missing shingles and the henhouse and the outhouse and my vegetable garden and the pasture and Frederick's trailer and the windbreak and see all the way across the rolling miles of cornfields to the grain elevators and the steeple of the Zion Lutheran Church, sticking up through the treetops in the town of Mount Olivet, and all the way to where the clouds bunch on the horizon, and I'd call out in my crow voice for all the world to hear the shame of our sins, the sins of this family and, God forgive me, me.

Chapter 2

1927

I lined up the knives and forks and spoons beside the four heavy white china plates, all the time keeping my back to my mother so she wouldn't see *Jane Eyre* inside my blouse. "Mutti," I said, "when can I cut my hair?" Every morning she combed out the tangles and braided my heavy red-brown hair into plaits down to my waist.

"Such a notion. Why do you want to cut your hair?" Her own hair was yellow gray, pulled straight back from her thin face. She tied it up with a piece of string and twisted it into a knot at the back of her neck.

"Miss Miriam Benson's got her hair bobbed," I said, "and marcelled."

She looked up from mashing the potatoes in a pot on the cookstove. "Such silliness. Why can't you keep your mind on your work and stop fretting about Miss Miriam Benson?"

I liked the new teacher right away, the first day of
school that September, but I figured she'd have a hard time
handling twenty-three pupils in eight grades, all in one
room. Miss Miriam Benson wasn't much older than my big
sister Gerta and not even as tall as my brother Karl and
some of the other boys that sat in the back and cut up.
Miss Benson was a tidy lady, small-boned and pretty, with
dark hair, cut short and waved across her forehead. She
still wore her skirts down to her ankles—not the short,
flapper style Pastor Lennart preached against. And she had
shoes with tapered toes and raised heels, the first I'd ever
seen. She was most likely a little vain about her small feet
cause she owned four pairs of those shoes—black, dark
blue, tan, and, my favorite, *red*—to match whatever outfit
she wore that day. Such vanity was a revelation to a ten-
year-old farm girl like me that wore heavy brown high-top
shoes.

Miss Miriam Benson had a nervous way of blinking
her eyes when she got rattled and clearing her throat when
she got mad. It might take a while, but when she did lose
her temper, everybody, even the boys in the back of the
room, knew somebody was soon going to feel their father's
leather belt across their backside.

The white clapboard school sat on a quarter acre cut
out of Mr. Calvin Rainey's pasture, about a mile and a half
down the county road from our place. Dusty and muddy
by turns, the schoolyard was beat grassless from years of
tag and jump rope and run, sheep, run. A swing made out
of an automobile tire on a rope dangled from the one tree,
a stout Chinese elm. And close by, a rusty teeter-totter
shrieked and complained when we seesawed during recess. Out back stood two privies, one for the boys and one

for us girls and Miss Benson. The boys' leaned sideways from being pushed over every Halloween. We all knew who did it, but since they were the same boys that had to use the privy the rest of the time, I guess they had some sort of a right to push it over.

I was the only fifth-grader that year, so after Miss Benson had each one of us stand up and read out loud, she put me with Francie Matthews and Mabel Bent in the sixth grade. After that, whenever I was through with my ciphering and parsing exercises ahead of the others, Miss Benson laid her soft hand on my shoulder and smiled and said, "Here, Hannah, you might enjoy this," and gave me extra books to read, books that were her very own, that she'd brought with her from the normal school in Lincoln. One afternoon, I decided to take home the little brown book I'd just commenced reading so I could keep on after I got through with my chores.

Karl didn't come to school that day cause he was helping Vater pick corn. So I took my time and walked home real slow by myself that Indian summer afternoon with *Jane Eyre* by Charlotte Brontë tucked inside my blouse. Along the gravel road, the shadows in the weedy ditches were cool and blue. But the air was still and warm, and dust hung there like powdered sunshine. I walked past a stand of yellow cottonwoods by the dry bed of Turkey Creek and caught sight of our house in the middle of Vater's stripped cornfields. The front windows upstairs and down reflected shiny gold from the sun low in the west.

Once, I asked Mutti why we lived in a big house with so many shut-up rooms we never went into, and she told me the story of Mr. Cyrus Morton's mansion. It was sup-

posed to be the grand house of a country estate when it
was built, way back in 1887, by the man that started the
bank in Mount Olivet, nine miles on down the county
road. The bank almost failed cause Mr. Morton spent other
folks' money on his new house. He shot himself rather
than face up to what he'd done. So the place didn't get
finished, and it stayed abandoned for a long, long time till
Vater bought the house and the land at a tax auction before
I was born. From where I was, walking along, hugging *Jane
Eyre* to my chest, the house with its pointy gables and bay
windows and shingles like fish scales still looked like a
grand mansion, even though I knew better.

By the time I'd got close enough to read Vater's name,
HERMANN MEiER, painted on our mailbox by the side of the
road, I could see how the white paint on the house was
cracked and peeling off. Vater said he didn't have any
money to waste on keeping up appearances.

The barn out back of the house was losing its paint
too, turning from deep red to a silvery pink, a prettier
color, I thought. The henhouse, where I headed, was
newer. Vater and Karl built it when Mutti decided to keep
a big flock for eggs and Sunday chicken dinners. The raw,
rough-sawed lumber was still a pale yellow with dark
streaks and knots. There was a row of windows with little
panes along the front and a door on the side, open now so
the chickens could go in and out to the fenced-in hen yard.

It was my afternoon chore to collect the eggs and feed
the chickens and refill their water pans. The white hens
cackled and squawked and scattered and came back together again while I went from nest box to nest box, gathering the eggs into a dented kettle I'd got from the back
stoop of the house. Mutti was ready one time to throw it

away since it leaked too bad to mend, but Vater, in his Old Country voice, said, "No, ve vaste nothing here." I set the kettle down by the wire fence and tossed cracked corn around for the chickens. They flapped and tumbled over each other and tried to be the first to get the most. "So greedy, so rude," I said. "Did I ever forget to feed you?" I leaned over and looked right at the hen I called Rose cause she had a fat pink comb. "Did you ever go hungry?" She clucked and lifted her yellow foot and put it back down again.

It took me three trips to the pump, filling a pail with water and fetching it back with both hands. Vater wouldn't have a windmill to pull the water up from where it flowed deep under the ground. He called them Satan's steeples and said they draw down God's wrath in bolts of lightning. Slopping water on my thick shoes and stockings, I filled the pans. What made it even harder this day was doing my chores and keeping *Jane Eyre* from slipping out of my blouse at the same time.

I carried the kettle of eggs through the dusk to the house. In the kitchen, Mutti was already setting the table, one of my chores too since Gerta left to work in Mount Olivet. "Hannah, where have you been?" She slammed the drawer shut and dumped a clattery handful of silverware on the oilcloth tabletop. "Hurry up. Your father's already waiting in the back parlor, wanting his supper." Her lips thinned to almost nothing when she pressed them together.

After I was through setting the table, while Mutti was still busy with the potatoes, I ran out of the kitchen and up the steep back stairs and into the bedroom I'd always shared with Gerta. Now, she just came back to the farm maybe once a month for a short Sunday afternoon visit. I took the book out of my blouse and stuffed it under my pillow.

"Hannah! Vot are you doing up there?" That was Vater hollering. I hesitated, then went back down the stairs, getting ready to make today's apology.

All the next day I thought about the book, and soon as school was out, I ran all the way home. Nobody saw me go up to my room. I sat down on the floor in the bay and read and read the tiny print in the failing light from the three tall bare windows. The floor was hard, but I didn't care. I was thousands of miles away across the ocean in England with poor Jane Eyre in Mr. Rochester's dark and mysterious house. All of a sudden, I heard Vater shouting, "Hannah! Vere are you?"

I shoved the book back under my pillow and crouched down by the bed. It was almost dark now. I hoped he was just calling and wouldn't come up to see if I was truly there.

The sound of his boots on the stairs and the glow of the kerosene lamp he carried rushed ahead of him along the hall and into the bedroom. Vater's black anger filled the doorway. His beard and bristly eyebrows made him look like somebody in the Old Testament, like Moses in the big family Bible in the back parlor, Moses carrying the stone tablets marked with the Roman numerals of the Ten Commandments—"Honor thy father and thy mother"— Moses when he saw the Israelites dancing around the Golden Calf.

"Hannah!" He stood over me, tall as Mount Sinai. His eyes were like slivers of glass. The lamp and my face were little reflections in them. "You vicked girl, did you think I vould not find you hiding here? You cannot hide from your vater."

"But, Vater, I wasn't hiding." I backed up farther against the side of the bed.

"Do not lie to me, Hannah, und do not argue." The black beard quivered when he spoke. "Do not add villfulness to your sins. You are a vicked, lazy girl. You come from school und hide away instead of tending the chickens."

Oh, no. I'd forgot all about my chores. I *was* a wicked, lazy girl.

"You vill go out now und do your vork. You vill come back to this room mitout your supper und pray God forgives you."

"Yes, Vater." I put all the humility I could into those two words, trying to put off what I knew for sure was coming. He held the lamp up high with one hand and unfastened his wide leather belt with the other. I didn't have to be told. I laid myself down across the patchwork crazy quilt and lifted up the back of my skirt and pulled down my underdrawers.

The room had got chilly after the sun went down, and the swish of the belt fanned the air, and it made it feel even colder against the bare skin, till the smack of the leather brought out the heat from someplace way deep inside.

———————

Miss Miriam Benson rapped her desk with a ruler and waited for quiet. "As part of our American history project, all of you are to find out about your own family's history and write a theme about it. Ask your parents where they came from, where their parents came from. Your themes are due next week on Wednesday."

That night after supper, I helped Mutti clear the table. Vater was having his coffee. I asked him to tell me about our family's history.

"Vot do you mean, history?" He wiped his mustache with the back of his hand, the hairs on it black and wiry like his beard. "Vy do you ask such things? Ve have no history."

"But, Vater," I said, "I know you came from Germany with your mother and father."

"Ja, I vas a little boy ven ve come from the Old Country." Above the dark eyebrows, his forehead was white from always wearing a hat outdoors. "Ve lived in Davenport, Iovay. My vater vas a butcher und owned a slaughterhouse."

"Where did you meet Mutti?" asked Karl. Since summer, he'd lost the boy-softness in his face. His straight black hair fell like a knife blade across the corner of his eye. He squinted and deepened his voice when he talked, like he was imitating Vater. First whiskers looked like a shadow on his upper lip. Karl had got curious about the older girls at school and complained to me in a sort of angry whine on the walk home cause they weren't interested in him.

"Ve met at church, of course," Vater said.

I looked over at Mutti to see if she'd add anything, but she just kept on wiping off the oilcloth with the dishrag.

"And then you got married?" Karl said, real eager.

"Ach, such foolishness. Ve vas married. That's

enough for you to know." He shifted in his chair and waved for Mutti to fill his thick white coffee cup again.

I wasn't getting much help with my school theme. "Mutti told me already the story about Mr. Cyrus Morton's tax sale, but how did you come to leave Davenport? Why did you leave the city for a farm?"

Vater slammed down his cup, slopping coffee across the table. "Never you mind. I told all you need to know. Ve have no history. Ve have only our vork. Now you finish helping your mutter mit dishes." He got up from the table and left the kitchen. Karl followed behind.

I shifted the dish towel around, looking for a dry spot. Mutti rinsed the last of the supper dishes, Vater's cup, and handed it to me. "Hannah, why're you asking all these questions?"

"I just want to know about the family. Why does that make Vater so mad?"

"You got to understand life hasn't been easy for your father. He doesn't talk about it cause it hurts his pride."

I reached up and put the cup on the shelf. "What happened?"

"During the war, your father couldn't go to the army. He had a family to see to, Karl and Gerta and me and Father Meier, who was too sick to run the slaughterhouse." Mutti emptied out the dishpan and pushed her hair back with a wet hand. "There was lots of talk then about folks with German names being the Kaiser's spies and traitors to this country. Such nonsense shamed him, made him very angry, but he couldn't do a thing about it."

I hung the damp dish towel over the back of a chair by the cookstove. "Where does the farm come in?"

"The anti-German talk hurt business, so after Father

Meier died, your father sold the slaughterhouse and set out
to find a farm where he could raise his family without
interference from anybody."

"Then you came here to Nebraska and I was born?"

"Yes, and then we came here."

So I had my family's history. I got out my school copy
book and a pencil and sat down at the kitchen table to
write my theme about the slaughterhouse and spies for the
Kaiser and dead Mr. Morton's tax sale.

———————

Miss Miriam Benson gave my theme an A and stuck a
real gold star on it, right next to my name, Hannah Sophia
Meier. I was so excited, after school I buttoned up Gerta's
gray wool hand-me-down coat and ran all the way home
through the early winter twilight. The cold air made my
chest hurt, but I never slowed down, not even when Karl
yelled at me to wait for him.

Mutti wasn't in the kitchen. I called and called, but
she wasn't in the house. It finally came to me this time of
day she was most likely down at the barn, milking. I put
my family history theme, shining with its gold star, next to
the lighted kerosene lamp in the middle of the kitchen
table and went outdoors to do my chores before it got too
dark.

When I came back in with the kettle of eggs, Vater
was standing at the table with my theme in his hand, his
lips deep in his beard moving while he read. His black
brows almost came together, he was frowning so hard.
Karl was leaning against the wall by the back door, watch-

ing Vater. "You're in big trouble now," Karl said to me under his breath, half smiling.

I was confused. When I left Karl behind while I ran home from school with my gold star, he was the one in trouble for not turning in a theme. Miss Benson said she was going to have to speak to his father about Karl's behavior. That meant a whipping for sure, I figured. Now here he was, smirking at me and saying I was the one in trouble.

"Vot is this? Vot is this?" Vater was shouting and waving the paper in my face. "Vy have you done this, you vicked girl?"

His anger took me by surprise, and I stumbled sideways against the cookstove. The smell of singed wool made me jerk back, knocking over a chair by the table.

"Vot evil makes you vant to shame your vater before the vorld? Answer me!"

I knew he didn't expect an answer. I was still trying to figure out the nature of my sin.

"Vot happens in the family stays in the family!" I nodded. "That teacher, that Miss Miriam Benson, she is behind this, ja?" I shook my head. "Do not lie to me. She put you up to this. Now she vill tell und disgrace us all. Ach, how can I stop her?"

"You could think up some story to get her fired, and she'd have to go away," Karl put in, eager for Vater's approval.

"Always the big ideas, eh, Karl? Ven vill you learn?" Vater wadded up my theme and stuffed it in the firebox of the cookstove. He watched it flare up before he put the lid back on. Then he turned around to me. "Up the stairs till I decide vot to do mit you."

The bedroom was dark and cold. I left my coat on and pulled the crazy quilt off my bed and wrapped myself in it. I heard the deep rumble of Vater's voice coming from outdoors. I moved over to the bay. Through the window, I could just make him out when he started across the frozen mud of the barnyard and into the dark. A minute later, in the circle of light from the lantern in his hand, Karl set off after him but stopped and looked back down the rutted drive to the county road. Into the light walked Miss Benson, wrapped in her heavy plaid coat, a red wool scarf tied under her chin. I tugged at the handle and tried to open the window, to warn her, but it was stuck tight. In my panic, I'd forgot it was nailed shut. All I could do was look down and listen and pray—Lord God, please, please protect Miss Miriam Benson from Vater's anger.

I pressed my cheek against the cold glass and heard her say, "I need to speak to your father. Is he here?" Her words came out in little puffs of steam in the cold air.

"He's busy down at the barn." Karl made his voice deep and serious. "What do you want with him?" He put down the lantern and stepped closer to her. I could see his fist clenched at his side. Miss Benson didn't move.

"You know you haven't been doing your school-work." She cleared her throat. "Also, I had a report that you were peeking through a knothole in the girls' outhouse at recess today." The frown on Karl's face relaxed into a smile. He seemed to think what Miss Benson was saying was funny.

She cleared her throat again. "And I've had complaints from Teresa Kovacs and some of the other girls that you've been trying to take, let's just say, certain liberties with them."

I was sure Vater was going to whip Karl good for that last part about the girls, even if it was on Miss Miriam Benson's say-so. But instead of acting scared, Karl looked down at her and laughed. He put his thick hands on Miss Benson's shoulders.

"Karl, what are you doing?" She tried to shrug them off, but his hands gripped deeper into her coat.

"You do this whenever you want to. Why can't I? You touch me and everybody else on the shoulder at school all the time."

"That's just a friendly gesture."

He nodded. "This is just a friendly gesture." Now he was mocking her. "So is this." He leaned down and pushed his mouth against hers, and when she fought to get away, he held her head in his hands and pushed harder.

I stood by the window gripping myself in my own arms. I couldn't move or make a sound. All I could do was think, This is the first time I have ever seen a man kissing a lady.

When he pulled back, she was shaking and blinking her eyes. "Karl, stop! What will your father say?"

Karl laughed again. "He'll say any woman that wears red shoes with high heels and comes in the night to tempt a young fellow is asking for trouble." His hands moved, one at a time, from her head down to grip her arms. "He'll say you deserve whatever you get, coming here without being asked and seducing an innocent boy that's not even sixteen till next month. He'll say you're disgracing yourself and bringing shame on this family."

Miss Benson struggled, her hands on his arms, trying to break away. "Karl, let go." Her words were high and faint, like a little girl's.

"I will call upon the Lord, Who is worthy to be praised." Karl was bending his head back and shouting now, quoting Scripture while he shoved Miss Benson down to the ground. "So shall I be saved from mine enemies." But she twisted out from under him and tried to crawl away, to get back up on her feet. He grabbed her around the waist and lifted her up like a troublesome calf that had broke out of the pasture. "In my father's name, I am the arm of the Lord and the sword of righteousness," he proclaimed over Miss Benson's screams that weren't even words anymore.

Then they were gone, out of sight, and I stared down at the pale circle of winter mud around the lantern. I listened, but the night was still. I looked up the other way and saw Vater standing there in the barnyard. His breath was rising from his beard like smoke. His hands were shoved deep into his jacket pockets, and he was looking back down the drive towards the county road. I thought I heard somebody crying. But Vater never ever allowed anybody in the family to cry.

Chapter 3

1928

I slept with *Jane Eyre* under my pillow for months. After Vater gave me a whipping for not tending to the chickens, I couldn't open the book again without hearing, in my memory's ear, the tramp of his boots coming up the back stairs. So I hid the book away. Miss Miriam Benson didn't come back to our one-room school. *Jane Eyre* was all I had to remember her by.

Without a teacher, we had no school. Karl said he was glad. He'd just been marking time anyway till he was sixteen and allowed to quit and work the farm with Vater, but I missed Miss Benson and I missed school. Even after the first of the new year, 1928, when they got another teacher, Vater made it clear I wouldn't be going back. "I vill not have my family corrupted more. You stay in the house, Hannah, und learn how to be a good Christian voman." So I helped Mutti with the cooking and the milking, and I still had my other chores, the henhouse to clean and the chickens to feed and the eggs to gather every day.

Now that I didn't have homework in the evenings, Vater made me come into the parlor and read the Bible out loud to the rest of the family. Besides the kitchen and pantry, the back parlor was the only room on the ground floor of the house we used. Vater had nailed the doors shut on the rest. Mutti said there was a dining room across from the back parlor and another room at the front of the house she called the library. Behind the two sets of double doors on one side of the front hall was a parlor big as two rooms. Mr. Morton ran out of money before he could finish it.

After supper was over and chores were done, we gathered in the back parlor. The roller shades in the windows of the bay were pulled down. There were no curtains, not anyplace in the house. Vater called them wasteful foolishness. The parlor was my favorite room, cause on the walls lived tiny ladies in long dresses and men in knee pants. They met in the tiny flower gardens of the faded wallpaper I could get lost in if I stared at it long enough.

We carried chairs in from the kitchen, and I read out loud from the thick family Bible with real gold on the edge of the pages. The place where I'd left off reading the night before was marked with a white satin ribbon Mutti had embroidered on when she was a girl—GOD IS LOVE. Now she sat at the center table with me, yellow-gray hair unraveling from the knot at the back and hanging forwards around her face. Her pale eyes squinted while she darned socks or mended Vater's work pants and such by the light of the kerosene lamp.

Vater made Karl sit in a straight-back kitchen chair so he'd pay attention. Karl pulled it way over next to the black big-bellied stove on the hearth of the boarded-up fireplace. He sat there with his rough hands resting on the knees of his overalls and pretended to listen. The fire glowed through little mica windows in the door. The heat must've made Karl drowsy. Unless I was reading some blood-and-thunder Old Testament story, like David and Goliath, Karl's head soon dropped forwards till his chin almost rested on his chest and soft sleep sounds slipped out of his open mouth.

Across the room, Vater leaned back in his leather-cushioned Morris chair and rested his eyes, he called it, and nodded his head whenever I read a passage he thought was specially suited to our moral needs. Sometimes his lips would move down in his tangledy beard, and he'd say a few words after me in his deep, ragged voice.

"And thou shalt do that which is right and good in the sight of the Lord."

"Right und good in the sight of the Lord."

When I came to a troublesome passage—like Deuteronomy 10:16, "Circumcise therefore the foreskin of your heart, and be no more stiffnecked"—I'd look over at Vater, his eyes shut, waiting for me to read on, and I'd look over at Mutti, and she'd wrinkle her forehead in a frown and shake her head. No questions allowed. Soon I found out I could run my finger along the lines of print and reel off the words for minutes at a time, taking nothing into my mind, not even listening to what I was saying.

Just like Vater said one drink of whiskey would give you a taste for drink—and lead you down the path to the life of a drunkard—a couple of hours of reading every night, even the meaningless singsong of the begats, com-

menced giving me a taste for even more reading, but for
something besides the Bible.

When I pulled the door shut, the closet smelled like
mothballs and kerosene. The dresses and skirts and
blouses, all sewed by Mutti and handed down from Gerta,
hung over me like the branches of the weeping willow
down by Turkey Creek. I made myself comfortable back in
the corner, wrapped in the crazy quilt Mutti had pieced
just for me, and took up reading *Jane Eyre* again after all
those months.

Earlier, before I came up to bed, Mutti had sent me
out to check on the new batch of day-old White Leghorn
chicks in the henhouse. I lifted down the metal lantern
Vater kept hanging on a nail in the pantry. I lighted it with
a split of kindling, taking fire from the banked cookstove,
and went outdoors. The rain that fell hard all evening had
stopped. The air smelled like spring, all washed clean and
new. The moon had come up, and the barnyard was
dotted with little reflecting puddles, like fairy moons light-
ing my way.

The chicks huddled under the brooder hood where
the coal-oil heater warmed their yellow softness. The
sound of the door opening had set them to peeping and
shifting and crowding together. I had to be careful not to
make too much noise, or they'd panic and bunch tighter
and maybe smother themselves. The chicks soon settled
down, and I was just about to leave when I saw something
light and still in the shadows way over across from the
roosts where the sleeping hens lined up like fat pillows.

When I took my lantern over and bent down for a closer look, I saw the stiffened fluff was a dead chick. "That's what you get," I told it, "for leaving your family."

When I was a little girl, maybe four or five years old, and first helping Mutti, I tried to bury all the dead chicks. I made a whole little cemetery down by the garden before Vater found out. He said it was a waste of my time and blasphemous besides to treat animals like they had souls the same as folks like us. He told Mutti to toss the dead chicks to the hogs.

Now, I touched the dead chick with the toe of my muddy shoe but didn't pick it up. A little at a time, I inched the yellow heap across the dirt floor, through the straw and feathers and chicken droppings, to the far corner and back into the darkness underneath a nest box. It wasn't a Christian burial, but it wasn't the slops trough in the pigpen either.

When I walked back, the roof of the house looked silver-painted in the April moonlight. I wanted to build a tall, tall ladder and climb up to the moon and leave the mud and dead fluff and everything behind. Then it came to me. I had a moon ladder made out of words—the book under the clothes in my bottom bureau drawer.

When I came back into the house, I shut the kitchen door real easy and carried the lantern on up the back stairs quiet as I could so the family wouldn't hear me from where they still sat in the parlor. Karl and me weren't allowed to take lights of any kind—lanterns or lamps or candles—upstairs. Mutti was scared they'd get knocked over and set the house on fire. And Vater said, "You do not need to see yourself undress, und you do not need light to sleep."

I hid the lantern, turned way down low, in the bedroom closet. Clouds had come back to cover the moon. Indoors and out was black as Egypt's night. By feel, I put on my cotton flannel nightgown and crawled into bed, to wait.

It seemed like hours went by before I heard Karl and my folks climb the back stairs. Through my eyelashes, I saw Vater come to the doorway with the lamp in his hand and look in. The light moved away, and he and Mutti went on down the hall and into their bedroom, and I heard them shut the door. We youngsters weren't allowed to have doors. Our father had taken them off the hinges and carried them away. Vater said, "A shut door means you are doing something you know you should not. You vill be less tempted to sin mitout the door."

But the closet had a door. When the house fell quiet, I creeped out of bed and into the closet and shut the door. I turned up the flame of the lantern and settled down to read.

After a time, my eyelids got heavy. I laid down the book and leaned my head back against the wall. Just then, I heard a scratching and scrambling above me and a moan that raised the hair on my arms. I'd read about how Jane Eyre heard sounds over her head in the night, and here I was, hearing them too. Was there a crazy Mrs. Rochester up there on the shut-off third floor where Vater had forbade us ever to go?

I was wide awake now. I grabbed the wire bail on top of the lantern and opened the closet door. The moan sounded again. And the scratching, scratching across the ceiling. Back down the hall, snoring sounds came from the doorway of Karl's bedroom. Mutti and Vater's door was shut. The doors of the other rooms we never used were shut too and nailed up besides. I tiptoed, shielding the lantern's light with my hand. At the middle of the hall, the steps to the third floor went up next to the broad front stairway that we never much used. I wasn't truly scared, since I expected to find the door to the attic nailed shut, but at the top of the steps, it swung open when I turned the knob. On the floor in front of me were laying the two bedroom doors, Karl's and mine, stacked up, one across the other, gray with dust. I climbed over them and found myself standing in what must've been the ballroom when Mr. Cyrus Morton built his fancy mansion so many years back.

From what I could see, the room stretched the full length of the house. The lantern shook in my hand, and, just for a second, I wanted to hightail it back to my bed and pull the crazy quilt up over my head and all. But this was so much like a story in a book, curiosity wouldn't leave go of me.

The room smelled musty and sour damp. I took one cautious step forwards, and the scratching I'd heard before sounded louder than ever. Down at the far end of the long room, little lights flickered, red. I took another slow step. The lights moved off, scattering left and right, and I saw mice, the lantern reflecting in their eyes.

A white flutter, a sudden ghost, flashed in front of me! I caught my breath. I saw then it was a barn owl swooping down on the mice. It caught one. The mouse squealed and twisted in its claws, and the owl flapped away. I ran after it and found panes broke out in the gable window. Of course. The scratching had only been the mice, and the moan I'd heard before was nothing but a barn owl's hoot. My crazy Mrs. Rochester was a hungry night bird, and now it was gone, out into the blue chill of the dark.

I wasn't scared anymore. I walked to the middle of Mr. Morton's ballroom and turned up the flame in the lantern and looked around. Cobwebs filled the corners. Tarnished brass candle holders, like empty arms, dripped with cobwebs too. The broad wooden floor was woolly with dust. Footprints showed where I'd walked to this spot. The walls between the gables were covered with cloudy mirror glass. I saw my reflection over and over, a runty girl, going on eleven, with long red-brown braids and eyes like black holes in a face lighted from below by the lantern in her hand.

Before this night, the only ballroom I knew about was in a story we'd read at school. If I let myself imagine it, this could be the place where Cinderella waltzed with Prince Charming till the clock struck twelve and she had to run away home. The horses pulling Cinderella's pumpkin carriage turned back into mice, and here they were now, scurrying around someplace in the woodwork.

The only waltz I knew was the "Missouri Waltz." Miss Miriam Benson had taught us to sing it. I couldn't remember the words, so I hummed the melody under my breath and stepped around the floor the way I figured a dancer would, spinning and dipping, swinging the lantern around and making light sway and bounce off the mirror walls. I was getting dizzy and out of breath, but I didn't want to stop. I shut my eyes tight. Maybe, if I kept spinning faster and faster, I could turn myself into Cinderella and be beautiful like the pictures in the book. I'd wear a dress of silver lace. The skirt would be full and round like a haystack. And I'd wear glass slippers with tapered toes and raised heels. I'd have long blond curls and pink cheeks like Gerta. I'd be grand, grander even than the ladies in the parlor wallpaper.

No Prince Charming, though. Somehow, in my mind he was all mixed up with Mr. Rochester at his coldest and cruelest. It worried me. I couldn't help wondering—in the story when the waltzing ended, when the fairy godmother waved good-bye and the two of them went off together— what would the Prince do to Cinderella?

I kept my eyes clamped shut. Spinning and humming in Mr. Morton's ballroom, I pictured *my* Cinderella waltzing on and on, alone and happy. I'd dance in a golden ballroom sparkling with candles.

CLANG! The metal lantern hit something, hard!

I stopped, frozen, and opened my eyes, face to face with pieces of myself in a shattered mirror, a girl in a faded flannel nightgown. Her feet were black with attic dust, and her eyes showed back wide and panicky.

Oh, no. Dear Lord, what if Vater had heard the lantern hit the wall?

I quick turned out the lantern. Crouching down in the dark, I strained to hear if he was coming. The pounding of blood in my ears drowned out everything at first. Then I heard the distant thump of Vater's boots and felt again the sting of his belt on my backside and remembered how the last time was so bad I had to squat on the outhouse seat to pee cause I couldn't sit down. I waited, hugging myself tight to stop from shivering. Please, God. Oh, please. The heavy boot sound died away—or had I just imagined it?—

died away into the wild bumping of my heart. The beat slowed and faded till I could hear the scurry and scratch of the mice all around me and far, far away the hoot of a barn owl.

Chapter 4

1931

*T*hat summer, the White Leghorns gave us more eggs than I could've pictured back in February when Mutti told me she was planning a bigger flock with money borrowed from Gerta. When I gathered the eggs in the dented kettle, it took three and four trips a day. Mutti helped me wipe each egg clean, and we put them down in the cellar, where it was cool. She hoped to sell them in town, but she had to be careful not to let Vater know too much ahead of time. I never questioned why it had to be a secret. I'd learned well enough that Vater's pride was at stake when it came to his farm and his family.

That summer was 1931, and we were in the Great Depression, though nobody I knew called it that at the time. Corn prices were so low Vater had us feed most of his crop to the chickens and to the hogs, and pork prices got so low he couldn't sell a one. So he and Karl slaughtered the hogs and cured what they could, and we ate what didn't spoil. We couldn't afford to buy what we couldn't produce ourselves, no matter what. Mutti saw the eggs as a way to make some money.

That summer, Vater and Karl planted the windbreak. They dug volunteer scrub pine and box elders and other trees from the banks of Turkey Creek and planted them along the northwest side of the house, out beyond the drive and the henhouse. Over the years, the stunted trees grew up and thickened and made a barrier against the bite of winter wind and the eyes of anybody passing along the county road. But that summer it was still possible to see, through the spaces between the trees, somebody coming along the road.

Though I was almost fourteen and strong for my size, the kettle clear full of eggs got so heavy I had to carry it with both hands. That day, I'd overloaded it to cut down on the number of trips back to the house and was scared the top ones might roll off and break on the ground. "Out of my way, girls," I said to the clucking birds inside the fence of the chicken yard, "or I'll drop these."

A fat white hen, the one I called Jemima, stood her ground in front of me while the rest of the chickens moved away in their stiff, high-stepping way.

"Get out of my road," I snapped. It was nine o'clock in the morning, and the day was already so hot it was hard to breathe. My arms strained to carry the kettle of eggs, and my shoulders ached from the weight. I was in no mood to argue with a sassy hen. I kicked dirt at her with the toe of my shoe and yelled, "Shoo!" She skittered to the side, and the others flapped and scattered, and I hurried out the gate. I looked back through the wire fence at the flock and searched for the nasty one that'd stood in my way. The

Leghorns kept milling around and mixing themselves together in the heat and the dust till they all looked alike.

I crossed the dry, rutted barnyard to the house. Behind me, above the clucking and squawking of the chickens, I could hear Vater hollering at Karl, "Is not vide
enough. Dig more vider. More deep."

At the back door, I set the kettle down on the stoop to
turn the knob. I was bending down to pick the eggs back
up when I caught sight of something moving between the
trees—a black automobile coming along the road. A cloud
of gray dust, like a rooster's tail, followed behind. I heard
the automobile turn into the drive and come towards the
house. A young man that looked to be about Karl's age
was at the wheel. I just stood there like I didn't have good
sense. Nobody but family ever came on the farm.

Mutti came to the open kitchen door and said, "I'll
talk to him." She moved me out of the way so she could
pass. I wanted to see and hear this stranger that was brave
enough to risk Vater's black wrath for trespassing, and yet
I was all of a sudden shy, aware of my faded, too-big dress
—one of Gerta's castoffs—and filthy shoes without laces.
I'd taken them out cause the chickens pulled at them,
figuring they were worms, I guess. But he wouldn't know
that. Why should I care what he thought? To my shame, I
did. I hurried indoors and commenced cleaning the eggs
with a damp rag, watching Mutti and the stranger through
the kitchen window.

The young fellow wore a blue cotton work shirt. His
face was shadowed by a wide-brimmed straw hat, creased
more like a cowboy's than what farmers like Vater and
Karl wore. His hands rested on the steering wheel of the
black Model A Ford, and he smiled all the time he and

Mutti were talking. She stepped back, and he opened his door and jumped down from the car. They were coming into the house.

It was too late to get away. They walked through the door into the kitchen, and Mutti said, "Hannah, this is Jake Coryell. His father owns the creamery in Mount Olivet." I nodded and looked down, dabbing at the egg in my hand. Mutti lighted a candle she got from the pantry and led Jake down the cellar stairs. I could hear their voices rumbling under my feet, making shivers run up the insides of my legs. I couldn't figure out why this bothered me so much, why I wanted to run away outside. But the back door opened before I could get to it.

"Vot's that automobile?" Vater pronounced the big word in his Old Country way, like it was four little ones. He waved a dirt-caked hand towards the Model A. "Vere's he gone? Vere's your mutter?"

I pressed back against the sink. Before I could say a thing, Mutti yelled up from the cellar, "Hermann, wait. We're coming."

The two of them came in, each one carrying a pasteboard box of eggs. Mutti introduced Jake. "Gerta told them we . . . we got extra eggs," she told Vater.

I could see the workings of Mutti's plan. During Gerta's last Sunday afternoon visit to the farm, Mutti must've told my big sister to talk to the folks at the creamery and set this up without letting Vater know. If I could figure that out, so could Vater. I waited for him to let go his temper.

Instead, he wiped his dirty hand on his trouser leg and held it out to Jake, who set down his box of eggs on the kitchen table and extended his clean white hand to

Vater. They shook, and Jake said, smiling, "Nice to meet you, sir."

Vater didn't say a thing. Between the bushy beard and the frayed straw hat, his face was dark.

"You'll be doing us a real favor, Mr. Meier," Jake went right on, "if we can count on you folks on a regular basis. You see, my dad's decided to open an ice cream parlor in town, next to the creamery, and we're going to need all the eggs we can get."

Vater still didn't say a thing. Mutti looked down at the box in her arms and bit her lower lip.

"I'll be coming out to pick them up twice a week, if that's all right with you, sir. It's kind of a route. I already pick up from the Pecks and the Raineys. Mondays and Thursdays?" In the silence, he was commencing to eye the back door.

I couldn't stand it. There was Jake caught between Mutti and Vater, ready to leave and maybe never come back to the farm again. So I spoke up, even though I expected it would mean trouble for me later. "Monday and Thursday'll be fine," I said and picked up another egg to wipe clean. I could feel heat like warm syrup flowing from my scalp down over my cheeks. I kept my head down on my work and cut my eyes sideways to watch while Jake and Mutti went out the back door. Vater stood by the table, leaning on his fist.

"You know about this?" he asked.

"No, Vater," I said. "But it is lucky, isn't it? I mean, the hens are laying so much in spite of the warm weather, and now all the extra eggs won't go to waste"—I was rambling, scared to stop—"and other folks are doing it and so it must be all right and . . ."

"Hush, girl," he snapped. "I am no fool." He turned and stomped back out. My head fell forwards, and I let out the breath I'd been holding. By supper, I hoped, Vater would've calculated the money he'd likely get from the egg sales and feel better about what Mutti and me, what we'd done.

Thursday, Jake came by with empty pasteboard boxes to fill with eggs. I watched out the window while he talked to Mutti. I nodded when they passed through the kitchen on their way to the cellar and pretended to be busy washing dishes when they went back through and out to his shiny automobile.

Monday, I watched from the hayloft of the barn, where I'd been pitching down clean straw into the stall where we milked Jenny, our cow. My skin prickled from the heat and the hay—and from watching the cowboy hat go in the house and come out again.

Wednesday, I washed my hair outdoors under the pump in the barnyard, brushing it dry in the warm evening's fading light. Oh, how I wished I could cut my hair. "A voman has long hair, it is given her for a covering," said Vater, quoting Paul to the Corinthians.

Next morning, Thursday, I braided it into a single red-brown plait hanging down my back to below my waist. But when Jake came up the drive in his black Ford, I found some excuse for being away from the house. I watched him coming and going from the hayloft again till he was out of sight, down the county road, and I couldn't hear the *choff-choff* of the motor anymore.

The next Monday, Jake was early. He caught me crossing the barnyard, coming back from gathering a kettle of eggs. The weather had got hotter, over a hundred the day before, and he said he wanted to get back to town before it got too warm for the eggs. He offered to take the heavy kettle from me and carry it back to the house himself.

"No, that's fine," I said. I kept hold tight with both hands around the wooden handle. I truly wanted to let him, but I could see Vater over by the windbreak. His arms were folded across his chest, and his face was hid under his hat brim. I was sure, though, he was watching us.

The sun made me sweat and squint. In the shade from his white straw, Jake's blue-gray eyes looked cool, like rain. He kept smiling and trying to get me to let him have the kettle.

He put his hand on my hand. "I'll tell you what," he said, teasing, "you hold on to one side of the handle, and I'll take the other. Like Jack and Jill going up the hill to fetch a pail of water." He laughed, and I laughed with him.

Just then I saw Vater headed for us, taking long, angry-looking strides through the weeds. I took off running towards the house with Jake trotting alongside, asking what was the matter. "Nothing, nothing, nothing," I said, in time with the jostling, rattling eggs.

Indoors, out of breath, I set the kettle on the kitchen table. "I'll get the eggs, Mrs. Meier," Jake told Mutti, shutting the outside door behind him. He struck a wooden match and lighted the candle in the holder, like Mutti had always done before, and went off down the cellar stairs.

Mutti was bent over the cookstove, heating a flatiron. She looked at me from under her eyebrows. "What was that all about, you two running up to the house?"

I didn't want to lie to her, but I didn't know myself

what we'd done to make Vater so mad. Or why I'd felt like
I had to run away from him. I got very busy at the sink,
pumping water to wash my hands. I hoped Vater wouldn't
come into the house.

"Hannah?" Mutti turned around to face me. She was
frowning. Her shoulders drooped forwards under her
housedress so it hung away from her like a feed sack. "You
be careful," she said. "You're too young to understand
about what fellows want from girls like you. Temptation is
in the flesh, like Paul told the Galatians."

"Yes, Mutti," I said real soft. She was right. I didn't
understand. Jake teasing me, us laughing together, and the
warm, syrupy feeling—why were they so wrong? Where
was that written in the Bible I read to the family every
evening after supper?

I shook the water off my hands in the sink. "Jake's in
a hurry to get the eggs to town before it gets any hotter," I
said, rubbing my hands down my sides along my skirt,
smoothing it down. "I better go help him."

Mutti licked her finger and tested the iron with a
sizzle. "You remember what I said."

The brick-floored cellar was cool and mossy dank.
Jake had got through loading one box with eggs and was
filling a second. The candle sat on the work table next to
him. Its light reflected off the shelves of glass jars full of
Mutti's canned tomatoes and green beans and such. The
flame wavered when I stepped close to him, and the shadows shifted in the far corners. His cotton shirt was wrinkled and wet under the arms. But he smelled like something to eat, like milk and vanilla.

Jake straightened up and pushed his hat to the back

of his head and smiled at me. His hair was the color of corn silk and curled along his forehead where it was damp. He tilted his head, and his fair eyebrows moved up like he was asking a question. My finger went to my lips to signal silence. He nodded and leaned across the box between us. His mouth brushed my cheek, and I jumped back like I'd been slapped. I picked up the box of eggs and ran back up the steps.

I waited in the outhouse, peeking through a crack in the door, till Jake and his Model A were gone. I was ashamed and joyous. I wanted to sing and cry and run away and hurt somebody, all at the same time.

All afternoon, I thought about Jake while I did my chores. I even talked about him to the chickens. Mostly, I had a head full of questions. "What he did in the cellar, does that mean he likes me?" I said. The hens kept right on pecking at the yellow specks of cracked corn I was tossing on the ground. "That was a kiss, wasn't it?" They acted like they were too busy trying to get more to eat than anybody else to give me an answer, if they had one.

I got to thinking about Mr. Coryell's new ice cream parlor. I knew what ice cream was, though I never had tasted any, but I had a hard time trying to picture an ice cream parlor. "Does it look like the parlor in the house?" I asked the white hens pecking around my shoes. "I mean, without the faded wallpaper and Vater's Morris chair?"

I said to one of the chickens looking up at me from behind the water pan, "What difference does it make? I'm never going to see it." It made me so mad I threw a handful of corn at her.

———

Even after sundown, there wasn't a lick of breeze, and
the air outdoors was still and warm. Crickets sawed slow
and raggedy like they just didn't care. Over in the direction
towards Mount Olivet, heat lightning teased along the line
between sky and cornfields. I tried to sleep, but the bedroom was hot as Mutti's kitchen on baking day. The windows in the bay all three were nailed shut and always had
been. That was Vater's doing, never explained to me. My
cotton nightdress stuck to my arms, my legs, all of me. I
lay on my back in bed, smothering.

I lifted up the hem of the gown and fanned my face.
The moment of relief blessed my legs. I shimmied out of
my underdrawers. The fanning cooled my belly too. I sat
up and peeled the nightdress off over my head and tossed
it on the floor. I turned over my pillow and laid back
down. All over my body, I felt the cool sweetness of the
morning with Jake in the cellar. And it seemed like I was
floating.

I must've fell asleep. When I opened my eyes again,
the full moon was up, turning everything outdoors white.
My nightdress glowed like a white flower in the middle of
the black floor. The bed sheet under me was soggy with
sweat. In the reflected moonlight, I raised myself on my
elbows and looked down and saw bare skin glowing in the
night, the pale ghost of my thin feet and legs, my belly, my
new breasts—all the nakedness I'd been forbidden to look
on, always forced to dress and undress, to wash piecemeal
in darkness or under cover of bedclothes. And without
mirrors.

Vater allowed no mirrors. "Those who look in them
follow vanity und become vain und go out und become
heathen," he said, quoting Second Kings. I remembered

the mirrors in the attic and the way, three or four years back, I'd seen my face in them one time, just that once, and was too scared of getting caught to climb those stairs ever again except in my memory.

Anyway, the attic would be hot as Hell's own ovens tonight. I just wanted to peel my skin off like my nightdress and lay myself down pure and chill, with nothing left to feel ashamed about. I lay back and tried to bring to mind again the cool sweetness of Jake and the cellar. I wanted to feel that floaty feeling some more.

When I woke up a second time, I was suffocating. I needed water, cool water. I got out of bed and started towards my nightdress. Everybody's asleep, I thought. It's too hot to put that heavy thing on. I ran on tiptoes out into the dark hall and down the back stairs to the shadowy kitchen. I felt my way to the pump by the sink. It creaked and clattered when I worked the handle up and down, up and down, till the well water gushed out. I cupped my hand and drank and splashed my face. I splashed my arms and legs. I made my own rainstorm and rejoiced in it.

Out of the dark, a hand, a strong hand, gripped my arm. Another hand clamped around my other arm and lifted me, dripping and shivering, off my feet.

"Harlot, you cannot vash the sin of fornication avay mit pump vater." His voice came through the black.

I was lifted high in the air and dropped, face down, across the kitchen table.

"I saw you, you vicked girl." His hand came down with a loud whack on my backside. "I saw you plotting your sin mit that young tempter."

"No, Vater," I cried into the oilcloth.

Another loud whack with his open hand.

"Now I catch you in your nakedness, sneaking back from your midnight coupling mit the devil."

Another burning whack. And another.

Vater was breathing hard, quick and raspy. I'd been punished many a time before. I'd got whippings with his stinging leather belt. This was different. He was laboring, pushing the pain deeper than the flesh. But he was hurting himself too, every time he hurt me. He was fulfilling his father-duty, justly chastising me. That I *had* to believe.

———————

When I woke up in my bed at first light, it all seemed like a nightmare I was climbing out of. I rolled over on my back, and I wished then it had been just a bad dream. But the ache and the shame were real enough. And the blood, more blood than any whipping ever drew before. My nightdress was soaked and sticky. The beefy red stained the sheet. Vater was right, like always. I'd sinned in thought, even if not in deed. He'd punished me for what I might've done if I'd had the chance. Now this was God's judgment. He was punishing me too, letting me bleed to death. "Forgive me, Heavenly Father," I prayed out loud. "What a wretched sinner I am."

Mutti found me asleep on my knees at the side of the bed, my forehead down on my clasped hands. She pinched her thin lips tight and came back with a clean cotton rag for me to wear between my legs to catch the blood. Sunday afternoon, Gerta took me up to the room we'd shared before she went to work in town and sat me down on the bed and told me what the bleeding meant and how it was normal every month. I tried hard to believe her. But I was just sure it was God's punishment. Monday morning, Karl harnessed Maude and Ruby to the wagon and took the eggs in to the Mount Olivet Creamery, the way he'd do twice a week for years to come.

Chapter 5

1931

I hadn't been in Mount Olivet for almost three years, not since we quit going to the Zion Lutheran Church cause Vater got mad at Pastor Lennart about the Virgin Birth. The town looked different. The houses and the stores seemed like they were smaller and closer together. But the red-and-white striped pole in front of Mr. Kemp's barber shop was still twisting around and around and disappearing into the bottom and coming out the top. On down the block, the picture show had a big sign out front—*BROADWAY MELODY* with BESSIE LOVE. And the new ice cream parlor filled the store that had been a pool hall, right next door to Mr. Coryell's creamery.

I'd never been to town before on any day but Sunday. What surprised me most this Saturday morning was all the automobiles parked in front of the three blocks of stores along main street. "Ford Model T's and Model A's, mostly," Karl told me when we rode by in the wagon. Its wheels rattled over the brick paving. Maude and Ruby, Vater's horses, shied and shivered whenever one of the machines came chugging towards us on the other side of the street. In front of the lumberyard, Karl yelled, "Look, a brand-new 1931 Buick roadster," and turned on the wagon seat to watch the yellow auto go past. Karl was almost twenty and longed to get a job in town like Gerta and buy an automobile of his own. But Vater needed his only son to help him work the farm. Besides, he said, automobiles were machines of the devil. "God made horses," he said, "before men invented horseless carriages."

We turned up a side street and plodded along past house after house shining white this cloudless September morning. Flower beds spilled over with zinnias and marigolds, and elm trees spread across and shaded the street. We turned another corner into Fremont Avenue. Karl shouted, "Whoa!" and pulled back on the reins and stopped in front of the Leflers' place. Mr. Lefler owned the hardware store in Mount Olivet, and Gerta lived with the family and worked as a hired girl. The house was high-gabled, white with green shutters and window boxes full of bright pink petunias. Fancy wood turnings and geegaws trimmed the front porch. The redheaded Lefler twins, four-year-old Bonny and Will, hopped off the porch swing where they'd been sitting with Gerta and ran along the cement walk towards us. My sister hurried down the steps after them, calling, "Hello, hello," and smiling.

She helped me down from the wagon seat and wrapped her arms around me in a hug that took me by surprise. Though we'd shared a bedroom all those years before she moved to town, we never had touched, not

once. It wasn't the family's way. I just stood there, holding
on tight to the brown paper sack with my nightgown and
hairbrush inside, and let her hug away. It felt odd and a
little scary, but nice at the same time, like I'd found something I'd forgot was lost.

Up on the wagon seat, Karl ducked his head and hid
his face under the raveled brim of his straw hat. "I got to
go," he mumbled, "got to stop by Gettscheider's Feed
Store and pick up ground oyster shell for the chickens."
He shook the reins and clucked at Maude and Ruby. We
all said good-bye while the slow wagon moved down the
street. The Lefler youngsters jumped up and down and
waved and hollered till Karl turned the corner and was out
of sight.

"Let me look at you, Hannah," Gerta said, stepping
back and holding me at arm's length. I looked at her too.
Since leaving the farm, she'd filled out in a womanly way,
and at nineteen she was the prettiest person I'd ever
known. When she smiled, her cheeks went round and
rosy, like wild apples. Her bright blue eyes and yellow
curls made me think of how Mutti must've looked before
she married Vater. "Come on," she said. "Let's get in out
of this sun. It makes freckles."

I followed her up the walk and tried not to look at the
freckles on my own thin limbs. Below her short sleeves,
Gerta's arms and wrists showed smooth and white.

Indoors, the house was cool and dark and filled with
the yeasty smell of bread baking. When we came into the
kitchen, Mrs. Lefler wiped her hand on her apron and
shook mine. She was short for a grown-up lady, about my
own height, and round like youngsters draw a snowman,
three circles with little dots for eyes and a big, half-circle

smile. "My, Hannah," she said with a sigh. "Why, you're almost as grown-up as your sister, aren't you?"

I nodded. Was I? I didn't know what to say.

Mrs. Lefler had on a housedress printed with big flowers and over that a red-checkered apron. You could see where the twins got their carroty curls—and their jolly energy. She turned around and put two more pans of risen dough into the oven. The stove was white and shiny and stood high on thin, curved legs, more like a piece of parlor furniture than a cookstove. I looked around for the bushel basket of cobs like Mutti had to feed the stove but didn't see any. How did they keep the fire going?

"Bonny. Will." Their mother waved little hands away from the loaves cooling on the table. "Behave yourselves now. We've got company."

Company? I was company? I was all of a sudden embarrassed. How was I supposed to behave? I'd never been anybody's company before. I looked at Gerta.

"Come on, Hannah," she said, putting her hand on my shoulder. "We'll get you settled, and then I'll tell you what I've got planned for you for your birthday." That was why I was there, why Vater was letting me spend a day and a night with Gerta, cause it was my fourteenth birthday.

In Gerta's room next to the kitchen, she took my paper sack and put it on the chest of drawers next to the matching comb and brush on the embroidered runner. Next to these, there sparkled a perfume bottle cut like a big diamond. Bonny and Will stood in the doorway, watching. "You kids go help your mom for a minute," Gerta said and shut the door. Her own room, her own door to shut, and perfume besides. I didn't have any notion from her now-and-then Sunday afternoon visits to the farm that she lived

in such luxury. "It is a sin against God's own Commandments to covet." I heard Vater's voice inside my head. But
envy, like a lump of raw dough, stuck in my throat.

"I've got two surprises for you," Gerta said. She giggled and bounced up and down where she sat on the bed
like she was the girl and I was the grown-up. "After lunch,
we're going downtown, and after supper, well, you'll just
have to wait and see."

"But, Gerta, don't you have work to do here for Mrs.
Lefler?" I was worried she might be punished or lose her
job cause of me.

"It's fine. Mrs. Lefler doesn't mind. She knows this is
a special day." Gerta got up and opened the door. Mrs.
Lefler was slicing a loaf of bread, and the little boy and girl
sat on the floor, pushing their mother's rolling pin back
and forth across the linoleum. "Here." Gerta handed me
an apron. "You can help us fix lunch."

The letters on the front window, lavender writing
with fancy curlicues, spelled out ARDITH'S SALON DE BEAUTY.
Gerta pushed open the glass door, and I followed her in.
The room smelled like ammonia and some sort of flowers.
A tall lady with hair the color of stove blacking looked up
from where she was shampooing another lady and nodded
to us over her shoulder. She was telling a story about some
fellow named Farley or Arley. It was hard to tell, since she
had a cigarette in the corner of her mouth and couldn't
take it out with her soapy hands.

I'd never seen anybody smoke before. "The smoking
flax He vill quench," Vater would've quoted Isaiah if he'd

been there. "He shall bring judgment unto truth," he would've told her and then probably saved God the trouble and quenched the cigarette himself. The way the smoke curled up and made her squint and the way the hot ash looked like it might drop off on the other lady seemed more dangerous than sinful to me.

Gerta steered me to a lavender-painted chair by a table piled with magazines and sat down next to me. All the way downtown, while we walked along the leafy streets, she shaded us with the silky blue umbrella she had rolled up in her lap now. She'd told me just farm girls let themselves be marked by the sun. Town girls boasted pale skin that meant they didn't have to work outdoors. Gerta had twirled the umbrella handle on her shoulder and said, "Men of means or promise favor girls who look like ladies." I looked down again at my own sun-freckled arms and was ashamed.

Gerta talked almost every step of the way, but her answer about where we were headed was a giggle and a roll of her eyes that made me laugh. Now we were sitting in the beauty shop, and I still wasn't quite sure why we'd stopped here.

"You'll see," Gerta said, sounding pleased with herself.

I looked around. I didn't have any idea what all the gadgets and machines and jars and bottles of colored water was for. Across from the shampoo sink was a padded metal chair that turned around when the lady with wet hair sat down on it. And on the wall in front of that was a big round mirror. Vater called mirrors sinful temptations to vanity. And, like always, I knew he was right. Soon our turn would come. I'd have to walk with Gerta to the back of the shop, and if I wasn't careful I'd see myself in that mirror. I decided not to look. I was going to shut my eyes so I wouldn't see how ugly I was compared to my sister.

When the beauty shop lady called Gerta's name, I kept my eyes down and watched the floor while Gerta's hand on my arm guided me to the padded chair and sat me down. I looked at the freckled hands in my lap. I folded them to hide the bitten nails. Somebody turned the chair towards the mirror, but I didn't look up. A piece of lavender cotton goods, like a tablecloth, was thrown over me and the chair, and fastened around my neck. I was scared. I squeezed my eyes shut and vowed not to open them or say a word till I got out of there.

"What's it going to be?" the lady asked.

"Ardith, this is my little sister Hannah, and she's never had a haircut."

I felt Ardith lift up the long, heavy plait at the back of my neck. "I can see that," she said. She let the plait fall and commenced undoing it. The tugging and stroking made my scalp tingle and gave me goose bumps. It was a strange new feeling, but not painful. In the dark, I could hear the *snip-snip* of the scissors and feel the teeth of the comb when it moved along my head and through my hair. I relaxed and forgot for a while to be afraid.

The two of them talked so soft I couldn't figure out what they were saying. After the clipping stopped, something hot pressed against my scalp while the beauty operator pulled and twisted my hair. The smell of burning, like singeing pin feathers on a chicken, made me wonder for a minute if I was on fire from the lady's cigarette ash. But I was too scared to say a thing.

"There, that ought to do it," Ardith said. And the

tablecloth was pulled off. I was left bare and all of a sudden cold. I opened my eyes and looked at the heaps of red-brown hair on the floor. That's my hair, I thought, the hair Vater said God gave me for modesty's sake. What will he say now? Worse, what will he do? Gerta had been away too long. She'd forgot what Vater was like when he was angry.

"Look, Hannah, look how pretty you are." Gerta was bent down in front of me, her hand under my chin. She was trying to get me to raise my eyes.

"No," I whispered so nobody else could hear.

She stood up and stepped back. I jumped out of the chair. Keeping my eyes lowered, I ran out the door and along the sidewalk. I turned into the first alley I came to, away from all the strangers and the reflections in store windows. Boxes and barrels were piled up at the back doors. The alley ended by the post office. I sat down on the stone steps and held my breath so I wouldn't cry.

The steps were hard and warm from the sun. High up, an American flag was hanging limp on its shiny pole. The empty sky behind it was so bright, it hurt my eyes. All of a sudden, I was covered in blue shade.

"Some birthday, huh, sis?" Gerta had walked up in front of me and held her umbrella over both of us. "I'm sorry, Hannah. I thought, well, I hoped you'd be glad to get rid of all that hair." She sat down and put her arm around my waist. "And you do look terrific, believe me."

I shook my head. It felt so light without the weight of my old plait. "It doesn't matter how I look. What about Vater? What's he going to do?"

"Nothing. I promise you." She tightened her arm around me. "He doesn't scare me anymore, and I won't let him scare you, either."

Could she do that? Was Gerta truly strong enough to stand up to Vater? She seemed so sure. I leaned my head against her shoulder and wiped my cheeks with the handkerchief she handed me from her pocketbook.

"Come on." She stood and tugged me to my feet. "Let's go start supper. I've got another birthday surprise for you after, one I can guarantee you'll like, okay?"

"Okay," I said. It was the first time I'd ever used that word. It felt good, just right, okay.

I washed and dried the dishes for Gerta while she gave Bonny and Will their baths in a big white tub upstairs —I was surprised to find out there was a privy up there too!—and got them into bed. Mr. and Mrs. Lefler sat out on the front porch, visiting with some neighbors. At supper, Mrs. Lefler had talked about my haircut, how the style flattered me, how grown-up I looked. "Don't you think so, Vernon?" she asked her husband. Mr. Lefler was a thickset, bald man with a gold tooth that showed in flashes when he talked. He nodded and agreed with his wife, then asked her, please, to pass the stewed apples. No matter what anybody said, I still didn't want to look at myself in a mirror.

About eight o'clock, Gerta and me were sitting at the kitchen table under the electric light, drinking lemonade, some of the same lemonade she'd just made for the Leflers and their friends out on the porch. Chunks of ice floated at the top and clanked against the glass when I tipped it up to take a cold, sour-sweet sip. Ice in big blocks was delivered three time a week to the icebox in the pantry. "And now," Gerta said, "Mrs. Lefler's even talking about getting an electric refrigerator that makes its own ice."

Somebody rattled the screen door on the back porch. Gerta patted her curls and smoothed her dress over her hips before she went to answer it. Back into the kitchen she came, followed by a man in a tan suit. He carried a light straw hat in his hand.

"Hannah," Gerta said, "this's Mr. Melvin Rasmussen."

I stood up. He looked like the sort of man folks stood up for, with his long, fine hands and wire-framed glasses.

"Melvin's reading law with Judge Tatum." Gerta looked at him like he'd carried the Commandments down from Mount Sinai himself. "One day very soon he's going to be a lawyer."

"Happy birthday, Hannah Meier," he said and held out his hand.

I shook it and couldn't think of what to say and then said, "Thank you." All of a sudden, I felt scared. What was he doing here? Did I do something wrong? Did Vater find out about the haircut and set the law on me?

Gerta slipped her arm through his and smiled at me, and I relaxed a little bit.

"Hannah wasn't too pleased with my surprise this afternoon, Mel. What do you think of her new hairdo?"

"Very becoming," he said and put his hat on the table. "Any more of that lemonade left, Gertie? Or would you young ladies rather walk downtown for a cone at the ice cream parlor?"

Mr. Coryell's ice cream parlor. I'd daydreamed about it all summer, but I never figured I'd get to go there. Would

I see Jake maybe? In the cellar, his lips had touched my cheek. Remembering that now made my whole face blush hot.

"Would you like to go, Hannah?" Gerta was already rinsing our glasses in the sink. The water ran hot or cold at the turn of a handle, another one of the miracles in the Lefler house.

"Yes. Please," I said. I hoped Jake would be there, and then, remembering my haircut, I hoped he wouldn't be.

At the door of the ice cream parlor, I stopped and let Gerta and Mr. Rasmussen go ahead. I looked around the bright room for anybody I might recognize from church or from the country school where I went till I was ten. I looked for Jake too, but all I saw was strangers, men and ladies and youngsters sitting at little round white tables on white chairs that looked like they'd been twisted out of heavy baling wire. Along both side walls, paper ivy vines framed—oh, no—mirrors. For a second, I couldn't move.

My sister was waving at me to come ahead to the table where they'd pulled out chairs. I looked down at the gray floor and made my way between the tables and chairs to where Gerta and Mr. Rasmussen were sitting. I kept my eyes down and nodded when Gerta suggested a dish of vanilla.

Mr. Rasmussen went away and came back a few minutes later with glass bowls filled with what looked like little snowballs. I took a spoonful into my mouth. The cold made me shiver, but the taste was sweet and rich, like the batter I licked out of the bowl when Mutti baked a cake.

Gerta said, "Thank you, Mel. This is delicious." She

patted her lips with a paper napkin. I wanted to do the right thing, so I did what she did. But I forgot myself and looked up when I thanked Mr. Rasmussen and caught sight of a face in the mirror next to his shoulder. I blinked and stared and tried to figure out who she was. Her hair was bobbed and marcelled in waves.

"Miss Miriam Benson," I heard myself say.

"Yes," Gerta said, "that's who you look like. I remembered how you used to beg Mutti to let you cut your hair like Miss Benson's. I told Ardith to fix it like that."

I blinked again. The reflection shifted. It was Miss Miriam Benson's hair, yes, but underneath it, I could see now, there was a freckled face with eyes like a stray cat cornered in the barn. And behind that, I caught sight of a young man coming across the room—Karl, it looked like. I quick shut my eyes.

What was he doing here? Vater must've found out about the haircut and sent Karl to take me back to the farm. My vanity would be punished, and I'd never get to visit Gerta in Mount Olivet ever again. I dropped my forehead onto my folded hands. I wanted to pray for forgiveness. All I could think was if I got up right that minute and ran out the door, could I escape? Where could I go Vater couldn't find me? Nowhere.

Gerta said, "What's the matter, Hannah?"

"Karl," I mumbled into prayer-folded hands.

"Where?" She touched my arm. "What're you talking about?"

I could feel him standing there behind my chair. Dear Lord, I told myself, I'm never going to get away from him, not ever. I dropped my hands and faced him in the mirror. Now I could see his hair wasn't black at all but more like the color of corn silk and curled along his forehead. His fair eyebrows moved up like he was asking me a question. I turned around in my chair and looked up at him, at Jake, who was grinning down at me.

Chapter 6

1931

$\mathcal{D}$aylight showed in thin lines around the roller shade behind the sheer white ruffly curtains. The house was quiet. Gerta was still asleep next to me. Outside the window, sparrows, it sounded like, chirruped and twittered in the morning glory vines. Back on the farm, the rooster would've crowed hours ago, and nobody lay in bed after daybreak. I shut my eyes. I didn't want this time to end. It was sweet with the memories of yesterday, and most of a whole day with Gerta was still ahead. All my fears and frettings were like something I'd almost forgot about from a long while back.

This must be what Heaven's like, I thought, everything becoming but not yet come and gone, happiness that lasts and lasts. Flowers budded and ready to bloom, Mutti's orange daylilies just opening came to mind. I pictured trees in bloom like the apple trees in Mr. Calvin Rainey's orchard, frosted white in the spring. But Heaven's a place

61

filled with all you could want of fruit, isn't it? How could it be both? I'd never thought about such matters before. But then I'd never known such earthly comfort and abundance before.

So what's it going to be? Wouldn't there be looking forwards and hoping, along with perfection, in eternity? And where was God in all this, besides standing off to the side and picking who gets in and who doesn't? This was more complicated than I could figure out. What does the Bible say? All I could remember at that moment was Matthew 5:12—"Rejoice and be exceeding glad, for great is your reward in Heaven."

Gerta shifted on her side of the bed, and I opened my eyes again. She turned her head towards me and smiled. "Good morning, Hannah," she said. She stretched and yawned and folded back the covers. Off a hook in the closet, she took a rose-printed wrapper and pulled it on over her lacy pink nightdress and tied it around her waist. When she raised the window shade, I blinked at the light shining through vines and white curtains.

I watched from my warm nest in the bed while she undid the knots of cotton rags in her hair and brushed out the yellow curls. Her skin was so smooth and creamy white. She reminded me of the hand-colored picture of an angel in the big family Bible back on the farm.

"Where is everybody? Why's it so quiet?" I asked.

"The Leflers sleep late on Sundays." She yawned again, covering her mouth with the back of her hairbrush. "Besides, it's my day off."

A day off was one of those notions I'd run into for the first time on this visit to my sister. She'd worked for the Lefler family for five years, but it appeared to me she didn't have to do very much that seemed like work. All Gerta did was help Mrs. Lefler with the housekeeping and cooking and watch after Bonny and Will when they weren't with their folks. And to have a whole day to do what she liked, that seemed like Heaven too.

Gerta left the bedroom, and in a little while I could hear her in the kitchen, opening cupboards and splashing water and humming what I finally figured out were hymns. I recognized some of "How Great Thou Art" and caught a bit of "In the Garden." After a few minutes, she leaned in the open doorway and smiled. "Come and have some breakfast," she said.

I got up and stood by the bed. My bare toes curled and uncurled on the soft braided rug.

Gerta stood with her hand on the door jamb and looked puzzled. "What're you waiting for?"

"Shut the door, and I'll get dressed," I said, holding my flannel nightdress lapped double across the front with my skinny, sun-freckled arms.

"It's just me, sis." Gerta laughed and took me by the shoulders and steered me to a chair by the kitchen table and told me to sit down. A green bowl piled with oranges glowed in the middle of the table, and I could smell their fruity sharpness. She handed one to me. "Here," she said, "peel this for yourself while I fix your eggs." Then she went over to the fancy white cookstove and struck a wooden match and lighted a fire under the frying pan.

I worked my thumbnail under the skin and licked off the tart-sweet juice that dripped out. Oranges were Christmas treats on the farm. When I saw them heaped in front of me and give away so free, I was amazed again at the generous bounty of this house. No wonder my sister had softened and got generous herself till she didn't behave quite like our family anymore—more like a Lefler than any of the Meiers I knew of.

Over cups of coffee, Gerta told me how good the Leflers had been to her. "They'll be coming down soon, Hannah, and I've got something I want to tell you. First, you like Mr. Rasmussen, don't you?"

I nodded. Yes, I did like him. He'd walked Gerta and me downtown last evening and treated us at Mr. Coryell's ice cream parlor. Mr. Rasmussen opened doors and pulled out chairs and acted towards my sister like she was the Queen of Sheba herself.

"Mel loves me and I love him," she said, easy as you please, without a bit of embarrassment. The word *love* was in the Bible, but I'd never heard anybody in the family say it on their own before.

"He's asked me to marry him, and I said I would. What do you think of that?"

It wasn't really a question, just a way of saying she was happy and wanted me to be happy with her. All I could do was put on a smile and wonder what Vater would do when he heard about all this.

I broke off a slice of orange. "When?" I asked.

"Next Saturday at Zion Lutheran Church."

"So soon? And you know how Vater feels about Pastor Lennart," I fretted.

"Never mind. It's Melvin and me getting married, not Vater." Gerta had either forgot how powerful our father's anger could be, or she'd got to be strong-minded as he was during her years in town. "I won't let him spoil things for me."

Brave talk. I envied her.

"Mel and me, we're going to tell Vater when we take you back to the farm this afternoon. I'm not afraid of him anymore. If he doesn't want to come to the wedding, that's okay. I'd like to have the family there, but I'm marrying Mel next week, and nothing's going to stop me."

I could see from the way she stuck out her chin and the tight line of her mouth she meant what she said.

"Two things I want you to do, Hannah." She set down her cup and took my hand in hers. "I want you to be my maid of honor, to stand up with me at the wedding."

I didn't know exactly what that meant, but if Gerta wanted me to, I'd do it, no matter what Vater said. Some of her bravery was rubbing off on me. Excitement was crowding out fear. I squeezed her hand a quick yes.

"And after we're married, we'll be moving into the house Mel's rented for us over near the courthouse. I'll be giving up my job here, and Mr. and Mrs. Lefler want you to come and take my place. Would you like to do that?"

Leave the farm and live with the Leflers? In this big white house with electricity and running water? I wanted to jump up and shout yes, yes, yes. But I couldn't. My bravery was wearing thin. "Vater," I said, holding tight to Gerta's hand. He was bound to say no.

"You leave him to me," Gerta said. "He's got used to the money I've been sending him to help out every month, and he won't want to try to make do without it."

I knew I shouldn't let myself hope, but I couldn't help it. I was already hoping, imagining myself in this kitchen, cooking and baking and doing the dishes with hot water coming right out of the tap.

———

After our noontime dinner, Mr. Rasmussen drove up in a dark green automobile and stopped in front of the Lefler house. His 1928 Plymouth coupe was three years old, bought used, Gerta told me, but he kept it washed and polished like it was brand-new. I followed her down the sidewalk to where it waited. I'd never ridden in an auto before, never even been this close to one, though Jake drove his father's Model A Ford out to the farm when he used to come to pick up the eggs.

I must've looked scared, standing there, clutching the paper sack with my nightdress inside.

Mr. Rasmussen laughed. "Come on, Hannah. No more horse and wagon for you. We'll take you home in style." He had on a blue necktie the color of Gerta's eyes. His hat was tipped to the back of his head, and he couldn't seem to stop smiling.

I stepped down off the curb and walked to the front of the Plymouth to get a good look at it. I circled around the dark machine, stopping at the back, curious about the extra wheel fastened there and, above that, a shiny handle.

Mr. Rasmussen reached over and gave the handle a turn and pulled down something like a door. "This is the rumble seat," he said. "Would you like to ride back here? Or inside with Gerta and me?"

"The rumble seat," I said, liking the sound of the words, "please." I felt very grand to have the seat all to myself after he helped me step up and in. Mr. Rasmussen held the door for Gerta and climbed in on his side of the automobile. The engine caught with a bang, like a gunshot. I let out a little squeal and dropped my paper sack onto the floor, but the *chug-chug* of the machine drowned me out. We pulled away from the curb and rolled along under the leafy elms and past the white houses and flower beds and on down Fremont Avenue, leaving the Lefler twins with their mother on the front porch steps, all waving good-bye.

Faster than Ruby and Maude ever could've galloped, we motored along the brick main street of Mount Olivet. I twisted around in the rumble seat to hold on to the picture a little longer while we passed the ice cream parlor. Last night, I'd talked to Jake for the first time since midsummer. He only got to stay at the table with Gerta and Mr. Rasmussen and me for a few minutes. His father expected him to help behind the counter, scooping up snowballs of chocolate and vanilla. If I lived with the Leflers, maybe Jake could be my beau, the way Mr. Rasmussen was Gerta's.

Please, dearest God, I prayed after losing sight of the ice cream parlor, let Vater tell Mr. and Mrs. Lefler yes.

We left the brick street and turned onto the gravel road out of town. We rumbled over the wooden floor of the Catfish River bridge and speeded on between weedy ditches and fields of sweet clover ready for the last cutting.

The wind blew my new-bobbed hair back off my face. I felt like I was flying. No wonder Karl wanted so much to get an automobile.

Overhead, the sun from early morning had disappeared, and the sky was like the inside of a tin washbasin. At noon, when we were all sitting down together around the big table in the dining room, Mrs. Lefler had remarked on the sky change. "More dumplings, sonny?" she interrupted herself to ask little Will. While she buttered a slice of bread for him, she said, "We sure could use some rain. The garden's parched. Maybe we'll get a shower."

But Mr. Lefler shook his shiny bald head. "Nope, not rain clouds, Flora. Dust." He'd reached for the bowl of sliced peaches. "Summer of drought and the fool farmers plowing after harvest just makes it worse."

Vater always plowed under the dry stalks in his fields after the corn was picked. He said it gave him a jump on spring planting. Windy fall days, swirls of dust followed him and the horses and the plow. Could Mr. Lefler be right? Was Vater doing something wrong? I was ashamed of myself for even having such a notion. Mr. Lefler might know hardware, but it was Vater's farm, and he knew about farming. Didn't he?

Now while we sailed along the gravel road, I turned around to get my face out of the wind. Behind us trailed a thick cloud of dust raised by the wheels speeding along. I turned back around. Through the auto's rear window, I could see between Mr. Rasmussen and Gerta. Beyond, in the road about a quarter mile ahead, a wall of dust along the next rise seemed to be moving towards us. The next thing, we were in it. Mr. Rasmussen slowed the Plymouth to a crawl. Around us, the wind whipped and the dust billowed like smoke. I leaned forwards close to the window and put my hand over my nose and mouth and tried to breathe between my fingers. All of a sudden, out of the gray fog ahead shone two lights—another automobile coming right at us!

Later, when I tried to tell Mutti what happened, I couldn't account for the time between the two lights and the pain in my head. What first woke me up was the wail of an auto horn, falling lower and lower till it stopped. In the quiet, I opened my eyes. Queen Anne's lace and sumac and dusty milkweed stood up tall around me. There was a bitter green smell coming from the weeds crushed underneath me. I looked up, and all I could see was gray sky. Only it felt like I was looking down into a well of dirty water. My head was confused and aching. The air was dead still. And then from far, far away, I heard Karl calling my name.

Chapter 7

1931

*M*r. Rasmussen was dead. So was Mr. Calvin Rainey in the other automobile. Karl carried Gerta in and put her down on the black horsehair couch in our back parlor. She couldn't move her legs or speak. Dr. Freeman Davies came from Mount Olivet and said we'd just have to wait and see.

Mutti tried to get her to eat something, but finally, after a day, she said, "Hannah, you try." So I heated up some chicken broth and broke some bread into it and took the bowl into the parlor, where she was laying under the faded gray afghan like she was asleep. "Gerta?" I said, soft as I could. Her face was dead white. I wanted her to open her eyes and be Gerta again, to cry or scream or do something, anything, to show she was still the sister I'd found in Mount Olivet. I wanted to put my arms around her, and I wanted her to put her arms around me and say again with her Sunday morning sureness that everything was going to be okay. I wanted her to tell me how she wasn't scared of Vater and how she'd protect me from his righteous punishments.

I dipped the spoon into the bowl and held it out towards her. "Gerta, please take just a taste," I said, loud enough to be sure she'd hear me. Her eyelids fluttered, but when they opened, she just stared at the ceiling. I coaxed and pleaded with her till she opened her lips and swallowed a sip of broth. That was a start. The next few days, she took a bit of whatever I brought to her. Still, her eyes stared, blue and empty, and she laid there, silent as snow.

Dr. Davies came back out to the farm to see her every day till he said there was nothing more he could do. It looked like Gerta was going to be crippled and have to stay in bed for good. When he heard that, Vater took a crowbar and hammer to the room down at the far end of the front hall. Long as I could remember, that room had been nailed shut. Vater pounded and wrenched and ripped all the wooden shelves down from the walls. His black beard and eyebrows got all speckled with plaster dust. He had Karl carry the shattered lumber out to the barn.

When he was through, Mutti sighed and brushed the stray hair back from her forehead. "Here," she said and handed me a broom. Mutti and me swept up the dirt and splintered wood and cleared out the cobwebs. I got some rags, and we washed the three tall windows that looked out on the drive and the new-planted trees in the windbreak. The top half of each window was cut in fancy beveled panes and put me in mind of diamonds.

When I got done, I stepped down from the chair I'd been standing on and looked around at the marks left on the walls. "All those shelves," I said. "Was this a big pantry?"

"No," Mutti said and wrung out her rag over the bowl of vinegar we were using to clean the glass. A sharp tang, like pickling time, hung in the still air of the room. "I'd guess this was Mr. Morton's library. The shelves must've been for his books."

So many books? I tried hard to picture that, rows and rows of books like the *Jane Eyre* that I'd hid years back in the bottom of my chest of drawers upstairs. But my imagination wasn't working too good since the accident. My thinking was too busy with what was real right here and now. All I could see along the walls was the scars from Vater's angry crowbar.

Karl fetched Gerta's old bed downstairs from the room we'd shared before she moved to the Leflers'. Now the family was back together again. But Vater was so furious about Mr. Rasmussen and Gerta he refused to come into her new room, and for the rest of his time, far as I know, he didn't say another word to his older daughter.

I lived in dread for weeks, careful of every move I made, just waiting for his anger to strike. Vater never said a thing to me, though, about how I'd gone against his wishes and got my long hair cut short while I was in Mount Olivet. Fact is, Vater didn't say very much to me at all but seemed to be always watching me from underneath his dark eyebrows. He kept a close eye on Karl too, like he figured Karl might manage to escape the way Gerta almost did, the way I almost did. Every Monday and Thursday when my brother hitched up the team to take eggs in to Mr. Coryell's ice cream parlor, I stopped wherever I was and watched. Vater was watching too.

"You see you be back here by noontime," Vater hollered after him when Karl shook the reins and Maude and Ruby moved down the drive.

I thought about talking to Karl and asking him to be my protector, now I'd lost Gerta. He was my older brother, almost a grown-up man, tall as Vater. But when he wasn't working alongside Vater, he was practicing to be like him, letting his frizzy new whiskers sprout into a beard and bossing me around every chance he got. Truth was, he had enough trouble getting away from Vater for a few hours each week himself. I finally decided Karl wouldn't be any help to me in my escape back to Mount Olivet and the Leflers' shining house. Besides, it was a sin to even consider such a thing.

As fall cooled towards winter, I worked out my penance. God was punishing me. Vater said so.

The Sunday morning after the automobile accident, the family, without Gerta, gathered in the back parlor. Since his falling-out with Pastor Lennart, Vater held his own Sabbath services. He wore his black suit jacket over his overalls and flannel work shirt and sat at the table in the center of the room with his coarse hands folded on the open pages of the family Bible. The rest of us—Karl, Mutti in the middle, and me—lined up in straight-back kitchen chairs. We sat like that for a time, waiting for Vater to commence preaching.

My mind wandered in the stillness, and my eyes fastened on the far corner of the room, way up at the ceiling where the paper curled back along the edge and was stained like the map of what Miss Miriam Benson had called the Dark Continent. The wallpaper men in knee pants and ladies in long dresses seemed to be doing a dance in Africa. I wondered, Is that maybe the waltz?

"Jesus spoke, saying . . ."

I was startled out of my daydream by Vater reciting in a low, calm voice the verse he'd taken for his text.

"Ye serpents, ye generation of vipers, how can ye escape the damnation of Hell?" His beard shook when he talked. His whiskers were going gray in streaks at the corners of his mouth. "Matthew 23:33," he added and stopped. His forehead was white and creased with a frown. He took a deep breath through his nose and let it out in a slow, raggedy wheeze. "Vipers, ja. Vipers is snakes."

I shivered. Of all God's creatures, I hated and feared snakes the worst. Once, when I was a youngster, I'd stepped barefoot on a garter snake while I was helping Mutti pick snap beans in the garden. I'd screamed and screamed till Mutti swatted me hard across my backside to make me stop.

"In the family are vipers vot bite the hand vot shelters them. They vait just to bite ven they can." He was staring at Karl, who, far as I knew, hadn't done a thing viperous or disloyal to the family, yet. "But God, He sees this. He knows this. Already, He has punished vipers, und he vill punish vipers again." This was a warning direct from God Himself to Karl. I was supposed to listen to it too.

"Take care you do not learn the vays of the viper." Now Vater had turned his head and was speaking right at me. I dropped my eyes to my lap and twisted in my chair towards Mutti. Her hand reached out, quick as a snake's tongue, to grab my knee and push me around again, facing forwards, facing Vater.

I could hear him turning the pages.

"Deuteronomy 32:22," he said and cleared his throat like he was getting ready to spit. "For a fire is kindled in Mine anger," Vater went on with no anger in his voice— more scary than the shouting I'd grown up listening to when he got mad—"und shall burn unto the lowest Hell." He stopped. The silence hurt my ears. "Do you remember ven ve vas burning off the veeds along the fence row, Karl? Und the flames found a snakes' nest, und ve see the snakes curling und burning in the fire? Do you picture, girl?" I nodded my head but couldn't make myself look up at his black eyes. "That is vot the vipers vill get for themselves." He stopped again. "Unless they repent."

Vater flipped the Bible pages back and forth, hunting for the passage he wanted. I watched him slantwise without lifting my head. "Second Peter 3:9," he said. He refolded his hands and leaned forwards. "The Lord is not slack concerning His promise, as some men count slackness, but is longsuffering to us, not villing that any should perish, but that all should come to repentance."

Vater scraped back his chair and got to his feet in a solemn way. He stood looking down at us like an angry God. His fists were clenched at his sides, but his voice stayed steady and low. "Hard vork is the earthly penance for sin. Hard vork and obedience. Und you vill vork, both of you, to earn God's forgiveness for your vicked villfulness." Then he walked out of the room, leaving Mutti to lead us in a final amen.

I was glad for the work to keep me busy. I took over most of the milking chores from Mutti, specially early in the morning, when the chilly air made her hands and knees hurt. She told me this like it was some terrible secret. We'd been taught, all of us, by Vater not to complain. So I milked and churned and washed up. I dunged out Jenny's stall and saw to her feed and watering. I shucked field corn and ran it through the hand-cranked machine to grind it up for the chickens. I cleaned the henhouse and put fresh straw in the nest boxes more often, maybe, than was truly necessary. Laying always dropped off some in the winter. I just needed to gather eggs once a day, but I spent as much time as I could doing it, talking to the chickens and staying out of Vater's way.

The flock and me worked things out—I talked, and they listened and pecked at the cracked corn and scratched in the dirt and kept busy with their own concerns. I knew Gerta had suffered terrible losses. I tried counting my blessings, the way the hymn tells you to. Mostly, though, I counted *my* losses. I'd lost Gerta to show me the way to be a lady with beauty shop hair and the pale skin a fellow might like. I'd lost the chance to live with the Leflers and find out about the world beyond the farm and the family. I'd had a peek at that world, and it wasn't all the Sodom and Gomorrah Vater made out it was. I wouldn't say it out loud, not even to the chickens, and it might be blasphemous to think so, but, Lord forgive me, maybe Vater was wrong about that, and other things too. I couldn't let myself dwell on that.

"I lost the chance to see Jake ever again," I said to the white hens fussing around the water pan. Memory warmed the cheek where his lips had touched it. And I remembered Gerta slipping her arm into the crook of Mr. Rasmussen's and the two of them smiling at each other the way they did on our Saturday night stroll along Fremont Avenue. "Now I'll never find out what it's like to have a beau," I said. I had to stop before the tears spilled over. The hen I called Ramona tilted her head and looked up at me, then went back to drinking. "A lot you care!" I screamed, taking the chickens and myself by surprise. The whole bunch went flapping and scurrying out the door and across over by the fence.

Of all that was lost in the accident, what I felt worst about then was the loss of hope. Never mind Heaven. Hope is the happiness that never dies, I decided, and losing hope is worse than never having any in the first place.

I stepped to the door of the henhouse and looked out. Karl was just climbing up onto the seat of the wagon where it stood by the back stoop. Mutti, in her thick gray sweater buttoned over her housedress, handed up to him a pasteboard box of eggs. I could imagine myself up there on the seat beside him. In front of me, Maude and Ruby would be swishing their black tails and shaking their heads and rattling their harnesses. A few more minutes and I'd be on my way down the county road and on into town.

Behind me, I heard one of the hens over in the nest boxes let out a cackle that sounded like somebody saying, "Fat chance."

I had to laugh. But I was so out of practice, it came out more like a rusty cough.

Maybe hope wasn't lost after all if I still had my imag-

ination, if I could still dream my secret daydream of escape. I just wasn't sure how to match that up with my
efforts at penance and the salvation of my immortal soul.

Evenings, after I got through with my chores, though
sometimes I was almost too tired to focus my eyes, I still
had to go into the parlor and read a little from the Bible
while Mutti and Vater and Karl listened. I raised my voice
loud enough so maybe Gerta could hear me too. When
Vater dozed off in his Morris chair, I went and lighted the
kerosene lamp in her room. I sat in a chair by the bed and
tried to bring back some of that sister-feeling we'd shared
in the faraway foreign county of the Leflers' kitchen. But
she kept her face turned from me and couldn't, or
wouldn't, speak.

So I did the talking, just like in the henhouse. I told
Gerta about the chickens and how they were doing and
what kind of day I'd had with Jenny. Once, I told her how
I'd fooled an old hen into laying again with a china egg.
Another time, I told her about the litter of three black-and-
white kittens I'd found in the hayloft. Their eyes had just
commenced to open. I didn't tell her they'd been abandoned by their mother—born too soon and runty, Mutti
said—or that I'd wrapped them in rags and put them in
the warming oven above the back of the cookstove, hoping
to save them. I didn't tell her either that they'd died in the
night while I slept or that I buried them under the tangle
of dried-up hollyhocks next to the back stoop. Instead, I
told her about the late squash I'd found down in the garden. And I described how, when I was coming back from

the barn at sundown, a sudden flock of pigeons wheeled up over the house and down out of sight behind it. The milk glass balls on the lightning rods glowed like twin moons. I didn't tell her the secrets I talked about with the chickens, but I told her about everything else I could remember, or could make up about the day, that I thought might entertain her.

Along about Christmas, one clear, icy morning, Mrs. Lefler drove onto the farm. She had on a red hat tilted to the side over her orangy curls. Mutti went out soon as we heard the sound of a motor coming up the drive. Vater walked up fast from the barn before Mrs. Lefler could get out of her automobile. She rolled down her window and handed Mutti a basket tied with a green ribbon. Mutti hurried back indoors. Through the kitchen window I watched, twisting my apron around my fingers. I couldn't see their faces, just the puffs of steam rising when Vater spoke. Did she ask about me? Did he tell her no, I couldn't come to work in town? Maybe Mr. and Mrs. Lefler didn't want me anymore. If they didn't, there wasn't anyplace for me to escape to, even if I figured out how to get away from the farm.

Vater stepped back from Mrs. Lefler's automobile, and she turned around in the barnyard and went back down the drive the way she'd come. I decided maybe I'd better give up fretting about the Leflers. I was getting pretty good by that time at not thinking about what I didn't want to think about.

Mutti said, "Hannah," and I turned away from the window. She held out Mrs. Lefler's basket full of oranges and plums and pears. "Take this to Gerta." When I got into the front hall, I did a wicked, selfish thing. I snatched off the pretty green ribbon and stuffed it down in my apron pocket.

The roller shades at the windows were pulled down, and in the gloom Gerta had her back to the door. "Look what the Leflers sent you," I said, cheerful as I could. She didn't need to know Mrs. Lefler was here and Vater had chased her away. That would just make her more unhappy. I stood beside the bed, peeling an orange for her. The tart sweetness was like that Sunday morning. Gerta turned towards me. Smiling, I held the first juicy piece out to her.

"Go away," she said, sharp as a slap in my face.

But the hurt faded when it came to me—Gerta was speaking again.

On our winter evening visits, more and more after that, she'd turn towards me and pay attention. Once in a great while she'd say a few words, maybe even ask a question about my day. Sometimes, though, I'd be talking along about the weather or the chickens, and she'd snap, "Leave me alone."

I felt empty as that china egg.

————————

When spring came around again, Gerta had some good days when she'd talk on her own. At first, it was mostly telling me to fetch this or that. Later, she'd sometimes recollect something that had happened years back, before she left for Mount Olivet—like the time when she was just a youngster and thought a skunk she found behind the corncrib was a kitty cat—and we'd visit for a few minutes and even laugh a little like two old friends. But the Leflers and Mr. Rasmussen weren't mentioned, and I never ever again heard her say the word *love.*

Chapter 8

1932

*T*here's a kind of light in winter when the sky and the snow cover are all one piece. It's a light so cold and white it doesn't cast any shadows, so flat it's hard to make out the depth and meaning of things, and you have to fall back on folly and faith. Every time I'm in that sort of light, it's 1932 again, and I'm crossing the barnyard through the drifted snow, coming back from carrying a bucket of boiling water out to the henhouse to thaw the drinking pans. The roof of the house is white like the sky, and no smoke rises from the chimneys. And in the winter light I feel myself turning from a fifteen-year-old girl into my own mother.

Late October that year, Mutti and me culled the old hens and worthless pullets from the good layers and cooked up the culls for canning. The kitchen was steamy for days, and several times when I'd look up from what I was doing, Mutti would be leaning against the table or a

chair with her hair stringing loose from the bun in the
back. The skin of her face was so tight and pale I could see
the bone underneath. She lifted a red-knuckled hand and
wiped her forehead with the hem of her apron.

Finally, I put down the carcass I was boning and
asked, "What's the matter?"

She waved away my question and went back to scalding the Mason jars in the sink. "You just tend to your work
there, girl. I'm waiting to process that batch," she said. But
her voice was softer than her words.

The next time I looked up, she was bending over the
sink. Her hands gripped the edge, and her eyes were
squeezed shut.

"Mutti!" I said and ran over to her.

She slumped forwards, and I grabbed her around the
waist so she wouldn't fall. "What's wrong?" I said next to
her ear. But she didn't answer.

I struggled to carry her into the back parlor and laid
her down on the horsehair couch. She felt so all of a sudden stiff and cold. I looked around for the afghan and
remembered seeing it last in Gerta's room. So I untied my
apron and spread it over Mutti's shoulders and tucked it in
around her chin. "Mutti?" Her eyes stared at me without
showing she knew who I was. "Mutti," I said, "it's Hannah." I took her hand and rubbed it between mine. She
blinked, but that was all.

I ran through the front hall to get Gerta, but stopped.
She couldn't help. Vater and Karl were out of doors someplace. I snatched Mutti's old gray milking sweater down
from the hook by the back door and ran out into the barnyard, yelling for them. I could hear the chickens over in
the henyard, squawking and flapping at the sound of my

voice. Pigeons fluttered into flight in the hayloft when I opened the barn door and hollered for Vater.

Please, dear Lord in Heaven, I begged, please let me find help for Mutti.

I searched in the barn, but all I found was Jenny with her warm animal breath rising in soft clouds. Maude and Ruby weren't in their stalls or in the pasture behind the barn, and the wagon was gone too. Where did they go, Vater and Karl? I tried to remember what Vater had said that morning at breakfast. My mind was twisted into a tangled knot of prayer and dread and panic to find help for Mutti. If we had a telephone like Mrs. Winona Rainey, I thought, commencing to get mad, I could've got hold of Dr. Davies. If only . . . if only . . . if only Vater wasn't Vater.

Such blasphemy! I was too frantic to let in the full shame of the notion.

And I wasn't helping Mutti by standing out there in the muddy ruts of the barnyard, hollering for Vater and Karl and getting back only the sound of my own voice off the house and the outbuildings. Just when I got to the back stoop, I thought I heard the creak and rattle of the wagon coming along the county road. I ran down the drive, shouting and waving at Vater and Karl and trying very hard not to cry.

By the time Karl fetched back Dr. Freeman Davies from town, it was too late. From outside the parlor door, I watched the doctor fold shut his black satchel. His eyes were made too big by thick glasses. He said, "Looks like a cerebral hemorrhage, Mr. Meier, a massive stroke." Vater banged the parlor table with his fist and got into a shouting match with the doctor. I covered my ears with my hands and ran and crouched down behind the cob basket in the kitchen, one of my hiding places when I was a little girl. From what I could make out, they were arguing about Mr. Horace Weber, the mortician in Mount Olivet.

"Law or no law," Vater yelled at Dr. Davies' back going out the kitchen door on his way to his automobile, "I am having no stranger touch my vife."

So it fell to me to prepare the remains for burial. I didn't have the least notion what to do. I'd never even seen a dead person before. Kittens, pigs, birds, maybe hundreds of chickens, but never a human being. I stood for a long time alone in the parlor, looking down at the thin body. Its eyes were shut in dreamless sleep. It didn't have any connection anymore with my Mutti. This was some frail, pinched-mouthed stranger.

I poured hot water from the kettle on the stove into a tin washbasin and stripped and washed the corpse, the only naked body I'd ever seen in full light. The joints poked through the blue-veined skin. The long toes twisted like crippled fingers. The breasts were wrinkled sacks, the nipples flat brown circles. The belly was sunk, and the hair down there gone gray white like old snow. With a shock, I saw this was the body I would have someday. It made me turn my head away. I prayed I wouldn't live that long.

I fetched Mutti's best linen tablecloth, the one she'd kept folded in the bottom drawer of the sideboard but never, in my recollection, spread on her table. I shook it out and pulled it up over the corpse.

I couldn't let myself think this was my mother. Mutti was someplace else right then, milking Jenny most likely, and she'd come into the parlor soon to see if I was doing this right, just the way she always checked on my work when I was doing chores. Since I was first big enough to clean the henhouse, to clear out the old straw and chicken manure and put down fresh litter, Mutti looked in every so often to make sure I did a good job. Any minute now, she'd walk through the parlor door and tell me what I was doing wrong.

But she didn't.

I went back out to the kitchen and found Karl sitting over cold coffee, both big chapped hands around the cup. He was holding on so hard his knuckles were white. His dark hair fell forwards, hiding most of his face.

"Where's Vater?" I asked. He didn't look up. I couldn't make out his answer. "What?" I said.

"I said, he's gone out to dig the grave." His bitterness took me by surprise.

From way down the hall, Gerta called my name. Oh, no. I'd forgot all about her.

By the light of the kerosene lamp turned low, I could see her eyes and cheeks were wet. For just a second, I wondered why. No need to mourn, I thought. Mutti isn't truly gone. I wanted to believe that.

Gerta was propped up in her wrinkled flannel night-dress. Her hair waited in tangles for brushing. The accident was more than a year back, and for the first time since, her cheeks had some color again, even if it came from crying. These were the first tears I'd seen her give in to since she lost Mr. Rasmussen.

I wanted to cry too, but I didn't dare. I took hold of

her soft hands and squeezed them tight. "Gerta," I whispered, "I'm through with the washing. What do I do now?"

"Her navy blue crepe dress," she said. "It's the nicest one she has."

I nodded.

―――――――

I never had been allowed in Vater and Mutti's bedroom that I could remember. The door was always kept shut. I opened it real slow and stood and hung on to the doorknob and looked around. The window shades were pulled almost all the way down. In the shadows, I could make out the high wooden headboard and heavy chest of drawers carved like rows of teeth. They looked like nightmare monsters crouching against the walls, waiting to jump out and eat me up.

I went and peeked over the footboard at their bed. This was where I was born. One side was flat and smooth, like nobody ever slept there at all. The other side had a deep furrow, big like Vater. The covering was a yellow-and-white wedding ring quilt pieced for her hope chest by Mutti when she was a girl my own age. Now it was faded almost to no color at all by years of washing in lye soap and drying on the clothesline in the sun.

The top of the chest of drawers was bare, like nobody'd ever lived in this room. I was scared to open any of the drawers. Some might be Vater's. I might find the leather belt he used to whip me with when I was a girl, before he quit work pants and took to wearing bib overalls.

God forgive me, but she'd just have to do without
undergarments.

Mutti's dress would be hanging in the closet. When I
opened the door, the smell of mothballs rushed out. A sour
sickness climbed up into my throat. I took hold of the skirt
of the dark blue dress and jerked it off the hanger and ran
out into the hall and pulled the door shut behind me.

Vater built the coffin from some of the shelves he'd
ripped off the walls of Gerta's room. The dark, satiny
boards made a fine show in spite of Vater's rough carpen-
tering. Karl helped him carry the empty box into the back
parlor and, with lid nailed tight, out to the front lawn,
where Vater had dug deep into the black loam. The rhi-
zomes of Mutti's daylilies were scattered through the pile
of dirt next to the grave hole.

I couldn't figure out what was the hurry. Though the
sky was low and overcast, there was still several hours of
late afternoon daylight left. I wanted to wash myself and
change into a clean housedress. I wanted Karl to carry
Gerta into the back parlor before they hammered down the
lid so she could see how I'd fixed the body in the coffin.
But Vater said, "Now. Come. It is time." So I did what I
was told and followed behind them, carrying in my arms
the family Bible with real gold on the edge of the pages.
The wind blew chill against my legs and raised goose
bumps.

The men lowered the coffin into the hole, and Vater
motioned for me to hand him the Bible. I did and stepped
back, far away as I dared. Standing on the other side, Karl

was about as tall as Vater and almost as heavy, but he seemed like a little boy, the way he pulled off his knit cap and wadded it up in his hands. Vater left on his sweat-stained gray felt hat. He towered over the grave in his wool mackinaw and overalls. He opened the Bible and held it in front of him with both hands. His beard was gray white with age and sawdust, and he looked like God Himself— silent and powerful and filled with wrath.

All of a sudden, he broke the silence. "Look down, Almighty, on this voman, my vife, I commend to You." This was his Sunday morning preaching voice. "Take her soul to live mit You in Heaven, vere she goes to make a new home for the family. This voman, my vife, vas a good voman, not mitout faults, but hard-vorking und no com-plaining."

The wind was blowing harder now, out of the north-west. The scrub pine and box elder in the windbreak whispered way back behind me. My feet hurt from the cold. I wrapped my arms around myself and tried not to shiver inside Mutti's old sweater.

"Merciful God," Vater raised his voice over the wind, "forgive the son and daughters of this voman for their sins, the sins vot broke this voman's heart und drove her to despair und death."

I looked over at Karl. His head was bowed, and his eyes were staring down at the coffin.

"Forgive the headstrong girl vot disgraced the family by acting the harlot. You have punished her vickedness by crippling her shameless body. You must forgive her. I can-not."

But Gerta was no harlot. I knew better than that. It was true she'd defied Vater as head of the family and God had struck her down. But what did she have to do with Mutti's stroke?

"Forgive the pigheaded boy vot thinks he is a man und vants to run off und desert his vater vot needs him, the boy vot vants to ruin himself in the fleshpots of the city und disgrace the family, just the vay his sister did. You must forgive him. I cannot."

Karl shifted from one foot to the other and twisted his cap in front of him. It looked like my turn was coming up next.

"Forgive the foolish, villful girl vot parades her body und lusts after young men und vould become a harlot und disgrace the family just like her sister if I vasn't here to stop her." He was getting louder and louder, fighting the wind. "You must forgive her. I cannot."

I shivered. Vater was shouting now and waving a fist at the clouds. His eyes looked towards the sky, and their whites shone out in his dark face. His beard streamed like a fierce banner in the wind. He seemed to have forgot Karl and me were even there.

"I cannot ask forgiveness for the doctor vot vould not save this voman, my vife, from such early death and vot vould vant to stop me from burying this voman, my vife, in her rightful place. He vould have her vait for Judgment Day in the Mount Olivet Cemetery mit all the souls vot have been sold by Pastor Lennart to the devil Satan."

I stepped away backwards towards the house. What was Vater raving about? Flakes of snow, sharp as flint, were swirling around us on the wind.

The pages of the Bible flipped and fluttered. Vater shook his fist over his head and shouted even louder, "Let all of them burn forever in the fiery pits of Hell!" He staggered back under the weight of his curse, and the Bible fell out of his hands and hit the muddy edge of the grave and tumbled in.

I let out a little cry.

Vater turned on me and yanked the sleeve of the sweater and pulled me towards him. He looked over at my brother. Karl's bare hands were shaking. "Hannah! Karl! Obey God's Commandments. Honor thy vater und thy mutter." He handed Karl the spade and motioned for him to fill the hole. He pushed me towards the pile of black dirt. He got down on his knees and took great big handfuls and threw them down onto the Bible and the coffin—the coffin of my mother. I could not pretend anymore it wasn't Mutti. She was gone, gone for good.

Thick snow was falling now. It was covering everything. I could see that and hear the wind, but I didn't feel the cold anymore. I just stood there and watched like I was made out of stone. I was hoping I'd turn into stone and stand over Mutti's grave always like a white marble angel in a cemetery.

Chapter 9
1932-1933

*T*ill the shooting, I didn't realize how much Vater had changed. It was like Mutti in her quiet, steady way had kept the machine of the family ticking along in clockwise fashion. When she was gone, the parts commenced going wrong and throwing the whole works out of kilter.

Without Mutti, I had Gerta's full care now, fetching her meals and washing her and dressing her and moving the way she lay in order to keep her from getting bedsores. Since I was with her the most, Gerta was the one I saw changing, and all for the worse. I never knew when I walked into her room whether she'd be sulking or out of temper or just plain mean. Mean times, her eyes squinted, and she'd tell me how lazy and stupid I was, till she wore herself down. Then, "Get out!" she'd yell at me, and I did. But when I couldn't stand it anymore, I yelled right back at her.

One time, she threw her hairbrush at me, but it sailed past my head and out into the front hall. I picked it up and tossed it right back. I missed too, and it bounced off the wall and onto the foot of her bed. We both just stared at it for a minute like we didn't know what it was, like it had dropped from the sky.

I got so put out sometimes I'd calculate ways to get even with her. When she screamed at me to fetch her something—a drink of water or the chamber pot—I'd leave and go through the kitchen and out the back door and slam it hard as I could so she'd be sure to hear.

Gerta was wearing me out. I still had the chickens and the milking and all of Mutti's work in the house to do. Finally, I decided Gerta needed to get out of that gloomy bedroom, some way, before she soured completely, and me with her. Even if she couldn't get up and walk, she needed to get out of that bed. She needed to see something besides four scarred walls and think about something besides her own miseries. So I went out through the bright winter morning to the stall in the barn where we stored odds and ends—bits of scrap metal and pieces of lumber and harness and such, whatever was of no use but we couldn't throw away. Like Vater always said, "Ve vaste nothing." It took a little wait for my eyes to get used to the dim light. Way in the back, I spotted the wicker carriage all three of us Meier babies had slept in till we outgrew it. Now it was covered with dust and cobwebs. We didn't need a baby carriage anymore, that was for sure.

I yanked and tugged it out from under a stiff piece of gray tarpaulin and a roll of rusty barbed wire, working the other things out of the way. In the middle of all the racket, a mouse ran out from under the pile of junk and scared me half to death. It kept going, up the wall and out through a knothole. When the dust settled and I had the carriage free, I worked the wheels and axles off, using a screwdriver and a pair of pliers. With a bit of oiling up, I figured, the wheels would work just fine.

Back in the house, I turned one of the kitchen chairs upside down and fastened the axles to the legs with big fence staples like Vater used to string barbed wire. Gerta hollered through the hall, "What's all that hammering?"

"Never you mind," I said. I turned the contraption rightwise and sat on it myself. With a good deal of squeaking and squealing, the wheels went around, and I scooted myself with my toes from the table to the cookstove and back. I grabbed hold of the table and pulled myself around it, hand over hand. It worked just fine.

Walking behind it and feeling pretty proud of myself, I pushed the chair down the hall and into Gerta's room. The roller shades were pulled down, like always, so a kerosene lamp burned on the chest of drawers by the bed. "Look what I brought you," I said, hoping she'd catch some of my cheerfulness.

She eased herself over on her side and scowled at me and then the chair. "What's that?"

"For you," I said and shoved it forwards. Its wheels chirped like metal birds.

"What am I supposed to do with that?" She was still frowning but the sharp edge had wore off her voice.

"You can get out in it, out of that bed. I can push you. Or you can work yourself around. You won't have to stay cooped up here all the time."

She stuck out her lower lip. She rolled back against

the pillow and folded her arms across her bosom. "Maybe I want to stay here. Did you ever think of that?"

I hadn't, but it didn't matter. After all my work, she was going to get into that chair.

"Here," I said, reaching under her arms and easing her towards the edge of the bed, "let me show you how it works."

"Take your hands off me!" she said in a low, cold voice.

I stepped back and put my fists on my hips. "So you get yourself onto the chair if you don't want my help. But you're going to get up." I was at the end of my string. "Make no mistake about that."

She stared at me. Her pale face was puffy with the weight she'd gained over the year and more since the accident. Her hair had got dark, the color of tarnished brass, and lost its curl. Just her eyes showed the spark and grit of the Gerta I remembered from Mount Olivet. "Okay"—she waved her hand—"push that thing over here next to the bed." She inched herself sideways and stopped. "Well, come on," she grumbled.

With her arms around my neck, I lifted her into the chair. She smoothed her cotton flannel gown over her knees. I could see she was pleased, though she wasn't about to say so. I wrapped the quilt from her bed around her and tucked the ends in so they wouldn't drag on the floor. I stepped back and smiled at my handiwork. "Now you can move yourself around, like over to the chest of drawers if you hang on to the bed. And maybe I can push you out into the kitchen later if you want me to."

"Get out!" she shouted, like I was already far away on the other side of the house. "Leave me alone."

A few minutes later, when I was in the kitchen, peeling potatoes for supper, I heard the metal birds chirping way down the hall.

Vater wasn't pleased Gerta could leave her room. When he heard the rolling chair coming, he always stopped whatever he was doing and got up and stood by the door. "You vill tell me ven the Whore of Babylon is gone," he'd say. That was my signal to stop Gerta before she got to where he was. Since he wouldn't let her eat with the rest of us, she had her meals at the kitchen table after Vater and Karl finished and went out of doors or into the back parlor and I was washing up their dishes. Always after dark, of course. She still had her foolish fear of sunlight.

It was like the two of them was on some sort of teeter-totter. When Gerta's moods showed signs of lightening, Vater's got heavier and more dark. I didn't like being caught in the middle. What could I do besides try not to upset either one? Helpless, I looked to Karl to mend things with Vater in some way. But Karl was turning into a bigger aggravation to Vater than either Gerta or me.

Almost every night, Vater and Karl argued at the supper table, usually about the work on the farm. Karl had ideas how they could improve things. Vater scoffed at him and, in the end, said, "No. Ve do like ve always do."

The worst fights, though, were about Karl's trips to Mount Olivet. He'd turned twenty-one, and he wanted to meet other folks and have himself some fun once in a while. Vater smacked his hand down on the oilcloth and denounced such foolishness and thundered, "A sinful vaste of time und money ve do not have." He wouldn't let Karl do a thing in town besides carry eggs to the creamery and come right on back.

During a long, cold stretch of several weeks, we were snowed in on the farm, and the hens were laying poorly. My biggest concern was just keeping as many of the flock alive as I could. We had no eggs to sell. Money was tighter than ever. To save heat, Vater shut the back parlor's double doors and moved the evening sessions to the kitchen. Since the big family Bible had got buried, we'd used Mutti's little one with the black paper cover stamped to look like leather. Christmas came without any celebration except me flipping forwards from where we were in the Old Testament and reading Luke 2:1–19. With no break in the weather, 1932 came to an end.

Karl got restless with no relief from his chores and no excuse for going into town. One icy Saturday night in January, he pulled a stiff, mildewed saddle out from the pile of discards in the barn and cinched it on Ruby and rode across the barnyard towards the county road.

Just before that, I'd been reading the Bible out loud till Vater dozed off with his head down on his arms folded on the table. Then I went upstairs and rolled up in my crazy quilt and crawled into bed with all my clothes on and tried to get warm enough to sleep. The insides of the windows were covered with frost so I couldn't see through, but the white light from outdoors made them glow like slices of the moon itself.

Far away, down by the barn, I heard horse's hooves clatter over the frozen ground. I sat up in bed, surprised and confused. I heard the gunshots, two of them! I jumped up and ran downstairs. I was shaking like the palsied servant of Capernaum. I stumbled out the kitchen door into the night, still clutching the quilt tight around me.

Since Mutti's passing, Vater had kept his .22 rifle in the kitchen, leaning against the corner by the back door. He said he had to keep it handy to scare off the sheriff or anybody else that might come and try to make him move her from the lily bed in the front yard to the town cemetery. Now, with the rifle in his hand, Vater stood over a black heap in the snow about halfway down the drive. I stepped back against the dark side of the house. In the frozen moonlight, I could see a big red pool forming at Vater's feet.

A scream came out of my mouth, like a little wild animal escaping. I tried too late to stop it with both hands. Vater turned and pointed the rifle at me. The crazy quilt slithered to the ground. I felt the sudden cold, but the shivering stopped.

—————

I couldn't sleep. The bedroom was dark now, and against the black I pictured Karl's face covered with blood. An hour or so before, I'd washed that face. His new beard was matted with frozen red. His eyes opened, and he looked up at me from the kitchen floor, where I'd dragged him. He managed a weak smile before he let go with dry, hiccupping sobs, like a scared little boy. I bent over him and patted his shoulder. "You're all right," I told him. "It's the horse Vater's shot. She fell and caught your leg under her. It's her blood you're covered with."

Karl nodded. He scrubbed his eyes with his fists. "Where's Vater?"

"I don't know. He stood over you for a long time, saying something I couldn't hear. All I could see was puffs of breath in the cold. After a long while, he walked right past me, back into the house, talking to himself like he didn't even see me there."

Karl was over the tears now. He frowned. In the light from the kerosene lamp on the table, his eyes were like black slits.

"I'm sorry you laid out there for so long," I said. "I had to wait for him to calm down and go back indoors before I dared go see to you."

Karl raised himself on one elbow and looked around the kitchen. "He was raving about Hell, I remember that. He's gone crazy, hasn't he?"

"Don't say that," I begged. "Please don't say that. He's our father. He's just mad cause you disobeyed him."

Karl shook his head and got to his feet and stood there, swaying. I grabbed hold of him and helped him upstairs to his bedroom. In the moon's light from the front hall windows, I could make out Vater's door was shut.

I went back downstairs and brought in the crazy quilt from outdoors and spread it out to warm in front of what was left of the fire in the cookstove. I knew what I was doing, I could see and hear, but I moved stiff and slow, like an engine that runs on fright.

I carried the kerosene lamp through the front hall to check on Gerta. It looked like she'd slept through all the commotion. I put the lamp back on the kitchen table and wrapped the quilt around me. I blew out the light and made my way up the back stairs in the dark to my bed.

But I couldn't sleep.

I was terrified of what Vater might do next. God for-give me, maybe Karl was right. Maybe Vater was going out of his head. What could I do? Gerta couldn't help me. I'd have to depend on Karl. I lay there, thinking about back when I was a youngster and how he'd been my hero and my protector. What came to mind was the time I crawled into the pigsty. A sow had just farrowed, and I wanted to play with the little pink piggies nursing at her teats. So I slipped between the fence rails, calling, "Here, piggy, piggy, piggy." All of a sudden, this huge fat animal covered with mud and manure struggled to her feet. She made these deep grunts and came trotting across the pen. I was surprised how fast she came towards me. Backed up against the fence, I was scared, yes, but I couldn't stop staring at her little eyes and her long eyelashes. Just when the sow was almost on top of me, a pair of hands reached down and lifted me up and over the top of the fence and set me down on the outside.

"She would've bit you for sure," Karl said, trying to make me see the danger I'd escaped, "maybe stomped you too." He picked me up and carried me across the barnyard to the back stoop. "You stay away from there now. If Vater finds out you upset his sow, he'll whip you good." He put his finger to his lips to show he wouldn't tell. And he didn't.

I got out of bed and felt my way down the black hall to his room.

"Karl?" I whispered at his open doorway.

It was too dark to see, but I heard him turn over in his bed. "Hannah?"

I walked forwards very slow, till my legs touched the

mattress. I leaned against his bed. "I'm scared, Karl. What're we going to do?" I felt his hand on my arm.

He spoke through clenched teeth. "He's a monster. I hate him."

I sat down on the edge of the bed. "Don't say that. God will punish you." I imagined a white-haired, white-bearded version of Vater with a white-hot lightning bolt in His hand.

"God's a monster, and I hate Him too," Karl whispered.

"That's blasphemy. Do you want to die and burn forever in Hell?" I commenced shaking again, expecting a wrathful God to strike down my brother right then and there. At the same time, I was glad to hear the strength in his voice. I needed a strong protector.

"You're shivering. Here," he said and moved over to make room for me underneath the blanket. I crawled in next to him and settled down into the warmth. For the first time since Mutti's death, I felt safe.

I must've drifted off to sleep.

What woke me was the scratch of whiskers on my face.

"Don't," I said, not sure if I was awake or dreaming.

Karl's lips were right next to my ear. "What'll you do? Call Vater?" He slid his leg over the top of mine. "What'll you say when he asks you what you're doing in my room?"

I tried to move away, but his arm tightened across my chest, and his knee forced my legs apart.

He laughed under his breath. I'd heard that vicious laugh before. In memory, I saw Miss Miriam Benson.

"I vill show him," Karl said, sounding like Vater.

"What do you mean?" I was panicking now. I couldn't untangle what was happening.

"Don't you get it, Hannah? He's just biding his time. He vants you for himself."

I tried to say something, but Karl put his rough hand heavy over my face. I had to struggle just to breathe.

Chapter 10

1933

With both hands, I held the axe up in front of his face. "Do you see this?" I said.

Karl was sitting at the kitchen table, waiting for me to put the coffee pot on and cook his breakfast. He twisted in his chair to look up at me. He scowled. I took one step backwards. I was still scared of him, even with a weapon in my hands.

An hour before in the gray near-dawn, I'd woke up back in my own bed, remembering the pain, like a hot poker. A deeper hurt told me it was my own fault for going in to Karl's bed and expecting any better. I made myself get up and go out in the cold to the barn and find the axe I used to chop the heads off chickens. I honed it nice and sharp on the whetstone till the new light ran along the blade like melting silver.

Now I held tight to the handle. "I'm sleeping with this next to me from now on," I said.

He folded his hands in front of him on the cracked, no-color oilcloth. "What're you talking about, Hannah?" With his head bent like that, his dark hair fell across, and I couldn't see his face.

"You know what I mean." I was fifteen and a half years old and small for my age and trying very hard to sound grown-up and tough as rooster meat. "I'm not going to let it happen again."

"You have a bad dream or something?" He laughed, not his vicious laugh but a second cousin to it. "Or are you going crazy too?" And he laughed again.

We're trundling along the county road. In the ditch weeds and in the milkweed and sumac along the fences, the crickets fiddle and sing. Grasshoppers leap and scatter when we pass. The sun's climbing through a cloudless sky, and the air's warm as dishwater. Corn plants stitch rows of little green knots against the black field we're passing. The rows weave across the slopes and down to Turkey Creek, running bankful with the late spring rain.

Gerta sits in her rolling chair. The wheels are crunching through the gravel of the road. She fixes the gray afghan around her shoulders and looks back at me and smiles. We waited for this day for weeks. First, the snows and cold weather kept us in the house, and then the heavy rains and muddy roads ruined our plans. But now, finally, we're on our way.

I figured it all out. It's nine miles into Mount Olivet. If I keep moving at a steady pace, we can be there, at the Leflers' house, before the light fails and Vater comes back in from the fields and finds out we're gone. What'll he do then? I wonder. When he finds the kitchen table bare and the cookstove cold, will he walk through the house, hollering at me to get his supper? Will he send Karl out to the henhouse and the barn to hunt for me? Will Vater go into Gerta's room? He hasn't been in there since he ripped out the shelves going on two years back. Most likely, he'll just look in at the door. When he sees the covers tossed back and Gerta's rolling chair gone, what'll he think? Who'll bear his rage then?

On the other side of the road now is Mr. Darwell Bent's pasture. The cows haven't been turned out into it yet this year, so the grass is going on waist-high in places and ripples in the breeze like a bed sheet when you snap it out and float it down over the mattress. Off a ways from the fence, a stock tank overflows, and the blades of a rusted windmill turn, clattering and creaking against a sky blue as Gerta's eyes.

Down in a little draw, a meadowlark warbles and trills from on top of a fence post. Its puffed-out yellow chest glows like a little feathered sun.

Coming over a rise, I catch sight up ahead of Mrs. Winona Rainey's apple orchard. The trees are like white clouds, and I feel such joy swell inside of me, like I could bust out into blossom myself. Oh, but all I can do is stop and point and say to Gerta, "Look at that."

And she smiles up at me and takes my hand in hers. "Beautiful," she whispers and squeezes my fingers.

"Beautiful," I repeat.

"Ow!" I cried—jerked out of my daydream. I looked down. One of the chickens had got up onto the window ledge in the henhouse and was pecking at the cracked corn

I was still holding in the palm of my hand. I tossed the grain across the dirt floor, and the rest of the flock scrambled to get at it. "Why couldn't you just let me keep going?" I snapped at her. "It was only a few more miles." I took a swipe at the white hen on the ledge, a greedy one named Freida, and she flapped down to join her noisy, quarreling sisters.

I leaned back against the rough wall and watched the dust motes dancing in the pale sunlight through the open door. My plans for our escape, Gerta's and mine, were still just plans, but this early March day was clear and warm, and it was time to commence getting ourselves ready.

I went through the kitchen and the front hall to her bedroom. In the lamplight, Gerta was propped up but dozing with her chin almost resting on her bosom. I touched her arm and said her name and moved back. Sometimes she woke up mad with her arms waving like a scarecrow in the wind. "Gerta?" I said again.

She lifted her head and looked at me like, for a minute, she didn't know who I was. Her face bunched into a frown. "What do you want?"

"Gerta, I got an idea. I want you to listen to me." She rolled over towards the other side. "Please, Gerta, don't turn your back on me. This is important. I thought about it for weeks, and I know how we can get away from Vater and back to Mount Olivet."

"We can never get away from Vater," she said and slumped back on the pillow and shut her eyes. But she couldn't shut me out.

"We can. We can go back into town and ask the Leflers to let us stay there in your old room. I can help Mrs. Lefler and take care of you too."

She opened her eyes. "Even if they'd take us in, how would we get there?"

"Walk," I said and folded my arms across my chest, gripping my elbows. Lately, my breasts had been growing and felt tender and strange, like they weren't really mine. I uncrossed my arms.

"I can't walk," she whined like a spoiled little girl. "You go without me."

"No, I'm not leaving with nobody to look after you. Karl couldn't and Vater wouldn't. Maybe you can't walk, but I can push you." I'd pictured it so many times I was sure we could do it. I reached for Gerta's rolling chair and wheeled it over beside the bed. "You hop into this, and I'll give you a practice spin around the barnyard. If we do this every nice day till the weather warms up for good, Vater'll get used to seeing us out there. Then when the roads dry up and the men are out in the fields, I'll push you down the drive to the county road and on into Mount Olivet." I stood back and grinned, proud of my plan.

Gerta lay there, soft and silent, her plump fingers twisting the hem of the pink-and-white patchwork quilt. I'd had hopes she'd be more excited about it, but at least she was listening.

"Besides, the fresh air and sunshine'll be good for you," I said.

Panic filled her watery eyes. I'd said the wrong thing. I'd forgot her old fear about what the sun would do to her skin. Who cared anymore if she got freckled?

"I'll wrap you up good," I promised her. "You don't have to worry about a thing. You'll see."

I begged and pleaded and tried every bribe I could

think of to get my sister to at least try an outing to the barnyard. That would be a start.

I wrapped her up in her old gray wool coat, all frayed and straining at its buttons, and tucked her around with the quilt. I tied Mutti's faded red calico sunbonnet on her head to shade her face. Gerta sat slumped and unhappy in the chair while I rolled it out the kitchen door and onto the back stoop.

She whined some more in her little-girl voice, "The sun hurts my eyes. And it makes me squint. I'll end up with crow's feet, and it'll be all your fault."

I tugged the sunbonnet down further around her face and tied it tighter under her double chin.

My next problem was getting the chair down the two concrete steps to the ground. I couldn't lift it, Gerta was too heavy. I couldn't just push ahead, she might be bumped and jostled out. I stood beside her and looked things over. I stepped down in front of her and eyed things from that angle.

"This is far enough," she pouted and commenced whimpering.

"Just hold on, Gerta." I went in past her and through the kitchen. The ironing board hung on a big nail on the back of the cellar door. I lifted it down and toted it back out of doors.

I laid the scorched muslin board down in front of her like a cattle chute. Gerta still wasn't satisfied. "It isn't wide enough."

"I know that," I said, just seeing the problem myself. "But if you lean over to your left so all your weight's on that side, I can roll you down on two wheels."

"Don't let me fall," she said. While Gerta fussed, I

lifted and pushed and held the chair back at the same time so it wouldn't tip or break loose and go rolling too fast. I finally managed to work the chair down from the stoop to the ground and set off on a little stroll across the barnyard, all to the rusty squeak of the carriage wheels. Our first stop had to be the stall in the barn where Vater kept a tin of axle grease.

The ground had froze and thawed all winter, finally drying into a crisscross of wagon wheel ruts pocked with footprints. It made for a slow, bumpy ride, but I kept on going. I shoved the rattling chair along and tried to soothe Gerta at the same time. "Isn't this nice? Why, this is the first warm day in months, and here we are, able to get out and enjoy it while other folks have to work." I was so busy trying to lift Gerta's spirits I was feeling pretty good myself. "Look at that." I laughed and pointed to where a row of gray-brown sparrows perched, facing us, on the sagging clothesline strung between the house and a winter-naked box elder. "We got an audience," I said.

Just then, the rolling chair pitched forwards and stopped, stuck, and Gerta slid to the ground and was bawling like a lost calf. I squatted down and tried to hush her. "Shhh, Vater'll hear you. Please, Gerta, don't take on so. You're not hurt, not really, and I'll get you back up in the chair and into the house before you know it. Just, please, don't make so much racket."

She quit howling, and we could both see what the trouble was. One of the wheels was busted off and bent flat on one side.

I stood up and looked around the barnyard, trying to figure out what to do next. A scud of clouds slid across the sun, and the air got chilly. Where was I going to find another wheel? I only took a couple of steps towards the barn when I saw the black shape in the double doorway. Vater must've been watching us all along.

The breath went out of me like I'd been punched in the belly. My legs turned to water. I half stepped back and sat down hard on the cold ground next to Gerta. I drew my knees up to my chest and put my forehead down on them. This is just a little hitch in the plan, I told myself. I'll get Gerta back to her bed somehow and find another wheel and wait till another nice day to try again.

Up above me, I heard Karl's gruff voice. "Come on, you two. I got better things to be doing."

I raised my head and saw him lift Gerta and settle her into his arms. I scrambled to my feet and followed them back into the house.

Later in the day, Karl fetched Gerta's chair back indoors. The axles and the other three wheels had been ripped off.

That night, the weather turned bitter cold again. I still hadn't got used to sleeping with the axe, even after a couple of months. It was always there, pressing hard against my arm or my thigh or my backside. All the while, I was half scared of cutting my clothes or the bedding or my own self on its sharpened head. But it was the only safety I knew how to make for myself. I turned and shifted and tried to get warm and settle into forgetful sleep.

That night after the wheel broke down, I lay awake for a long time, going over and over again the ways for Gerta and me to make it into Mount Olivet. I couldn't figure out how we could both do it without the chair, and Vater had fixed that. All I could think to do now was to wait for warmer weather and strike out walking by myself.

Once I got to town, I'd have to convince Mr. and Mrs. Lefler to help me rescue Gerta some way. I wanted to pray to God for His help in all this, but I wasn't sure but what He was, like always, on Vater's side cause he was head of the family.

I couldn't sort that out right now. For the moment, I needed to get to sleep. A full day of work waited for me in the morning. But something still nagged at me. What was I overlooking in my middle-of-the-night fretting?

Never mind. I turned on my side and nestled down into the bed next to the axe and conjured up the picture of summer and its heat so as to warm myself. The night of the terrible heat rose up in my memory's eye. I thought about my nightdress like a white flower in the middle of the black floor, the smothering room, the soaking sweat, the sticky blood—the blood! That's what I'd been trying to remember. How long had it been since the last of my monthlies? How long?

Oh, no. I tried to figure back. Not since Christmas? Not since the turn of the new year? Not since before the shooting.

———

We were standing in the kitchen by the back door. Vater had already gone out to the barn, and Karl was buttoning up his wool mackinaw. He said, "What're you talking about?" A dark frown crossed his face. Quick as it came, it was gone, and he laughed, like I'd just finished telling him a great big joke. He pulled on his black knit cap and tugged it down over his ears. "What's the matter, Hannah? You think you're the Virgin Mary or something?

The trouble is, you been reading the Bible for so long you got yourself believing the Holy Spirit's been in your bed." He turned to kitchen door and held it open a ways. A shock of cold air blew in. He looked back, dead serious now. "You really are crazy," he said and walked out.

Chapter 11

1933

Violets bloomed purple in a patch of green leaves next to the outhouse. When I came out and stepped closer, two butterflies, pale purple like sun-faded flowers, flew up together and flittered around and around each other like they were waltzing in the air. I held my breath so as not to scare them away. Some kind of music I couldn't hear was moving the two of them through the quiet May morning. They fluttered and climbed up slow, turning, up and turning, till I lost sight of them against the bright blue sky. Something in me flew up there with them, and I felt light as a butterfly when I walked back across the barnyard to the house.

Indoors, the kitchen was warm, and the air was heavy with stale cooking smells, last night's cabbage and last year's too. The chickens were tended to. Gerta was waiting. I poured hot water from the kettle on the cookstove into the tin washbasin and carried it through the front hall to her darkened room. I turned up the flame in the kerosene lamp. Gerta followed me with her blue eyes but didn't say a thing. Some days she was like that.

"I'm going to give you a little bath, Gerta," I said in my happiest voice, trying to jolly her into helping, "and then we'll put on your clean nightdress." She didn't look very pleased, but I went right on unbuttoning and pulling and working her flannel gown off over her head. I dropped it on the floor and wrung out the washcloth in the basin. "Here," I said, and handed it to her to wash her own face. She just laid there, staring at me, with her hair that used to be like yellow embroidery floss. Now it was just dull tangles.

We'd been through this many a time before. If she didn't want to help, I couldn't make her. So I wiped her face off, wrung out the cloth again, and went onto her hands and arms. Scrubbing away, I could see how fat she was getting, just laying in bed. Without the rolling chair, she never left her room anymore. It was a real job for me to move her around and lift her out and down onto the chair without its wheels. And then she just sat there while I straightened up her bed or changed her sheets.

Her skin was white, like bread dough, creased and folded at her elbows and wrists. I wrung the cloth out once more and commenced washing her near shoulder. She looked down at herself and pushed my hand away. "Here," she said, "I'll do that. I hate the way you look at me, I've got so big." Her voice was shaky with feeling sorry for herself. She took the wet cloth from me and dabbed away at her big, doughy breasts, like she couldn't hardly stand to do what she was doing.

I turned away and fiddled at straightening up the things on the top of the chest of drawers.

"Done," she said and handed the cloth back to me.

I rinsed it out and leaned across to pull Gerta over so I could wash her far side, but she wouldn't move. Instead, she reached her hand up and touched my belly. I jumped back and almost knocked the washbasin off the chair.

"Hannah?" Her eyes were serious. "Vater? Did he do this to you?"

I looked down at my own swollen body. I'd been wearing loose dresses, hand-me-downs of Gerta's, for weeks, trying to hide my shameful condition for long as I could. I shook my head and bit down on my lower lip.

"I might've guessed Karl would come after you if Vater didn't." Gerta's voice dropped to a whisper. "Mutti sent me to town, but you got to protect yourself, girl."

"I sleep with the axe in my bed," I told her.

"Too late, it looks like." She pointed towards my belly. "What's Karl got to say about that?"

"He acts like I'm lying or I dreamed this up and he didn't do a thing. He says it's my own fault."

Gerta nodded, and her lips twisted into half a sour smile. "That's how they work it, Hannah, so it's always our fault."

If Gerta knew about all this, about how they work it, why didn't she warn me before? Why didn't Mutti?

"But Karl can't deny what he did much longer," Gerta went on. "You're getting too big to hide. When is it due?"

I didn't know how to figure that out, and I was ashamed of my ignorance. I knew how long hens brood eggs and how long sows take till they farrow and cows to calve, but I didn't know a thing for sure about babies. My blushing must've told on me.

Gerta laughed for the first time in I couldn't remember how long. She asked when I had the last of my monthlies and calculated on her fingers. "Looks like early October from what you say. The worst part's going to be when Vater finds out."

I'd been dreading that worse than Judgment Day. "What can I do?"

"Nothing. Just do your chores and keep out of his way the best you can. It won't take Vater long to figure out who's the father. Let brother Karl look out for himself."

About this time, I had a dream. It was like a gift, from God maybe. I couldn't be sure where it came from, but it was mine now, and I'd come back to it whenever I lay in the dark too troubled by the day to fall asleep no matter how wore out my body was. Those fretful nights, I would recall that dream and think myself into it till sleep came and carried me away.

In my dream I am small again, a little girl all alone in the schoolyard. I sit in the auto tire swing, rocking back and forth in a lazy, soothing way. With my toes dug into the dusty hollow under the swing, I push myself higher and higher. When I look down, I am way up above the ground, swaying in a slow half circle in the thick, sweet air. I can see the leafy top of the elm tree and the wood-shingled roof of the one-room schoolhouse. Up, down, up, and I'm high over Turkey Creek and the pastures and cornfields it threads through. Way far down below, I can

make out the house, the henhouse and the barn, the corncrib and the outhouse, tiny like toys. Then I rise up
through a cloud of softness. And everything's white . . .
and pure . . . and perfect.

The wind whipped the white bed sheet back in my
face and wrapped its cold wetness around my bulging
belly. I shivered and stretched up on tiptoes and struggled
to hang the sheet on the clothesline way over my head.
The wooden clothespins stuck on the wet cotton and had
to be forced down tight, or I'd be out later picking up
muddy sheets. Then I'd have to wash them all over again,
simmering them in soapy water in the copper boiler on the
cookstove, rinsing them in the galvanized-tin washtub, and
feeding them through the hand-cranked wringer in the
sink—hard work that left my back sore and my hands red
as raw meat.

The sun was out, and once I got the wash all hung
out, the wind would dry it fast enough. I pinned the last
flapping pillowcase and walked back down the line to pick
up the empty washbasket. I was just bending over when I
heard Vater's voice behind me.

"Whore!" he shouted over the wind.

I turned around. The bed sheets waved like giant
white flags on both sides of me. They whipped and
snapped in the wind. His eyes were like two burning holes
underneath his hat brim and black brows. He moved
closer. "Whore!" he yelled at me again. The empty basket
stood between us. "Ven you vent to town, I knew vot vould
happen. Fornicating mit that young devil Coryell, ja?"

"But, Vater," I said. He kicked the basket out of the way and slapped my face before I could say another thing. It was going on two years since the last time I saw Jake. Vater had to know that. Was this how he was going to put the blame on me and let Karl off the hook? Gerta was right.

He grabbed hold of me by the shoulders. "Listen to me, harlot." His hands gripped hard and shook me like a rag doll. My breakfast climbed up to my throat. "Hell's fires vait to burn your flesh for vot you did, bedding mit the devil und bearing his evil spawn." He stopped. "Meats for the belly, und the belly for meats, but God vill destroy both of them like vot Paul told the Corinthians."

My head was dizzy. What was he yelling about? What did all that mean?

"The body is not for fornication but for the Lord, und the Lord for the body." He let go of my shoulders, and I teetered there, trying to keep my balance. "You disgrace the family," he said in disgust.

The sheets billowed out around us. He drew back his hand and slapped me again along the side of my head, so hard I stumbled backwards and fell on the ground. I rolled onto my side, my arm crooked under me.

Vater seemed like a giant in his gray felt hat and ragged overalls, big as Mr. Darwell Bent's bull. Vater scowled down at me with his hands in fists at his sides. His beard was streaked with white and quivered like it was a separate, living, angry thing. I looked down. The toes of his work boots were crusted with dried mud and manure and stood just a couple of steps from my belly. For the first time, I didn't think about how he might hurt me. All of a

sudden, I thought about the baby, about what he might do
to it if he kicked me with those heavy boots.

I begged him, "No, Vater, please," and rolled over
and out of the way. Just that minute, a gust of wind
whipped a bed sheet sideways, between us. There was a
loud cotton *snap!* And when it fell back, Vater was gone. I
sat up and looked around. My head ached so bad I
couldn't hardly make my eyes work.

Over on the other side of the upended washbasket,
Vater and Karl were wrestling on the ground—two heavy,
work-strong men rolling and pounding each other with
their rough hands. Karl's straw hat came off and was tumbled away by the wind. Vater banged Karl's bare head
against the rutted ground. Karl rolled over and took Vater
with him. The sheets fluttered and snapped. Chalky dirt
covered the men's clothes and beards, and the wind lifted
the dust they kicked up, like smoke full of deep, fist-
pounding grunts. They sweated and breathed hard, they
scuffled and hammered on each other. It was an even
match. Blood trickled from the corner of Vater's mouth
and out of Karl's nose.

At long last, my big brother had come to protect me
from Vater—or had he? I knew better now than to count
too much on that ever again. Maybe this fight didn't have a
thing to do with me or the baby. Red-faced, Karl seemed to
be paying Vater back for more than twenty-one years of
beatings and God-righteous tongue lashings—and the rifle
shots that had just missed killing him.

Better get out of here while I can, I told myself. I
scrambled up and ran towards the house. From behind me
came a bellow of pain, like the sound of an injured animal,
like the time Jenny's calf got kicked by one of the horses. I

turned back to see Karl standing over Vater, who was curled on his side, hugging himself, clutching his chest.

———————

Dr. Freeman Davies wrote "heart failure" on the death certificate. Karl had run down the road and asked Mrs. Winona Rainey to use her telephone and call in to Mount Olivet. When the doctor came, I stayed in Gerta's room with her. I blew out the kerosene lamp, and we waited, silent in the shadows. I could hear the two men's voices but not what they were saying. I sat in the wheel-less chair, my arms folded over my belly, scared Dr. Davies might come through the hall and see me and ask questions I didn't want to have to answer. Like Vater said, "Vot happens in the family stays in the family."

We all cried after the doctor left. I still haven't figured out why. Karl sat at the table in the kitchen, where the fire in the cookstove had gone out. He bawled like a little boy, and the tears ran down into his black beard. Gerta sat propped up in her bed, sobbing and carrying on worse than when Mutti passed on. And me, who'd always been scared of my father and scared of his connection with God and his power over every minute of my life, I went and curled up in the far corner of the dark parlor where Vater was laid out on the black horsehair couch and wept.

Chapter 12

1933

Skittery hens are one of the first signs. When I came out onto the back stoop after doing up the noontime dishes, I could hear the chickens clucking and carrying on, running back and forth and squawking like something was chasing them. Only, I could see there wasn't a thing out there, just the flock of White Leghorns, bunching up in the far corner of the chicken yard, squeezing up against the wire fence, then shifting back towards the henhouse and scattering, some indoors, some out.

The August afternoon was still and muggy. The sky overhead had turned a strange sort of lemonade yellow, and nothing seemed to have a shadow. I stepped down off the stoop and stood looking around, with my hands pressed into the small of my back. My ankles and bare feet had swelled with the heat. My old shoes without laces stood paired up by the back door for when I went out to do chores, but I wasn't sure if I could even get them on again today. The belly underneath my damp housedress trickled with sweat. The baby seemed restless as the chickens, pushing out what I supposed was a knee here or an elbow over there, trying to get comfortable. Comfort for myself was something I'd give up on several weeks back.

I lowered myself onto the top step. Next to the stoop and across the back of the house, clumps of spindly hollyhocks came up on their own, year after year. The flowers bloomed a faded, sickly pink. When I was a little girl, I used to pick the blossoms and set them down on the steps like fine ladies in long dresses and try to figure out what they'd say to each other at their fancy party, but there my imagination always broke down. So, in high, squeaky voices, I made them complain about how much we needed rain and how the grasshoppers and the potato bugs were eating their way through the garden and how the heat cut down on the hens' laying—Mutti's concerns then and mine now. Here I was, a girl not sixteen till next month, and I already thought like an old wore-out farmwife.

I reached over and broke off a flat, fuzzy leaf from a hollyhock. The stem oozed a sharp, peppery smell. I waved the leaf back and forth under my chin, fanning myself. The air stirred the loose ends of my hair pulled away from the bun at my neck, but it stayed hot as Nebuchadnezzar's furnace.

While my belly had got bigger, my arms and legs got thinner, till I must've looked like some kind of freckled spider. I was glad there was nobody around to see my ugliness besides Karl and Gerta. And neither one of them even mentioned my condition, though my sister's temper had sweetened a good bit, and lately she'd stopped throwing things and complaining about how slow I was.

Across the dusty barnyard, the chickens kept up their shifting and clucking. Karl was someplace out in the fields. Since Vater's passing, he'd somehow kept the farm running. With Maude in single hitch, he'd plowed and planted and cultivated. He did his own chores and Vater's too. And over the months, Karl had got more and more like Vater in the way he acted and in the way he talked. He took on for good Vater's German accent. He turned into the righteous enforcer of God's law, and the evening Scripture reading in the back parlor went on. Sometimes I'd be reading along and I'd look up from the page and stop, my breath dried up, at the sight of Vater come back to life. But it was just black-bearded Karl in the sallow kerosene light, dozing in the Morris chair.

I stopped my leaf fanning in midwave. Something wasn't right. The chickens' fretting had stopped, and they'd all disappeared inside the henhouse. No bees buzzed around the hollyhocks. No sparrows twittered in the box elder. No wild doves cooed on the barn roof. The stillness was like a thick green soup. From behind me, way on the far side of the house, I heard—and felt—a steam engine coming along the county road.

I heaved myself up off the stoop and went back indoors. "Gerta," I called out to her. Her room was dark, but I was too scared to light the lamp. I stood beside her bed, still holding on tight to the hollyhock leaf. "Greta," I said again, like she could save me, could save us all.

The bed springs creaked when she turned towards me. My eyes were getting used to the shadows. Her white face floated in front of my tight-stretched belly. "What's the matter?" Her voice sounded stiff with sleep.

"It's so quiet, and I heard a steam train—where there isn't any railroad tracks." No, that wasn't it. What was I trying to say? I couldn't think straight. All of a sudden, the word jumped out—"Tornado!"

The door in the kitchen slammed, and Karl ran towards us through the hall, his heavy work boots banging, banging, but I couldn't hardly hear them. It was like he'd let in a howling wind when he opened the back door. Across the room, the window glass rattled, and the roller shades swayed in and out, letting in flashes of gray light. Karl stood frowning in the doorway. When the daylight came and went, I saw his mouth moving in his beard. He stepped forwards and grabbed my arm. "Come on, girl," he yelled into my ear, "into the cellar!"

But I tried to pull away. "What about Gerta?" I said, loud as I could.

Her eyes were wide and shiny. She'd thrown back the top sheet and was trying to push and pull herself to the edge of the mattress. I moved to help her, but Karl jerked me back towards him. "No time," he said and cursed our sister. "Ve can't carry the old sow all that vay."

I hoped she couldn't hear him over the rush of wind.

"We can't just leave her," I shouted. Someplace over our heads, a crash shook the house, then the high shiver of glass breaking.

Light flashed again around the window shades, and I saw Gerta's face was washed with tears. Her mouth was open wide, and her tongue curled pink and wet under her scream. That terrible picture has always stuck in my mind over the years and bound me to her.

Karl grabbed me under the arms and moved me through the front hall. My feet never touched the floor till we got to the bottom of the cellar stairs. He pushed me into the far corner and crouched down beside me. I could hear he was panting like he'd been running for miles. And over the whoosh of the wind and rain and the rattle of hailstones against the stones of the foundation, I was sure I could hear Gerta calling out my name. A great crash shook the wall behind us and set the empty Mason jars on the shelves to chiming. We'd left her up there alone to die, and God was going to punish us by dropping the whole house in on us while the glass jars danced and rang.

I had a moment of helpless panic too at the thought of the chickens being tossed around by the wind like crumpled pieces of paper. Just then a pain stabbed my belly, like a sliver of the glass I'd heard breaking up above us. I let out a cry. I put both hands over my mouth. To my sudden shame, I commenced peeing a hot puddle where I squatted on the brick floor, and, no matter how hard I tried, I couldn't make it stop. When the pain came again, it was stronger than I was, and I gave out a holler louder even than the wind.

It came too soon, almost two months too soon. In the dark of the cellar, Karl, who'd helped with farrowing and calving since he was a boy, knew what to do, just from the feel. In the roaring blackness, I gritted my teeth and twisted the wet cotton of my skirt in my hands and pleaded with God—"Hear me when I call, O God . . ." I prayed, trying to remember the rest of the psalm, "have mercy upon me . . . Have mercy upon me, O Lord, for I am weak. O Lord heal me, for my bones are vexed." They were a whole lot more than vexed. I was too deep in pain to fear His wrath. Under my breath, I cursed Him for not heeding my prayers and not easing my suffering. Finally, after I don't know how long, it came sliding out in a hot gush. I was so tired out, I fell right to sleep, breathing through my mouth, thankful the pain was over. Later, I woke up and saw I was alone. A weak light shone from way up at the top of the cellar stairs. The sound of the wind had died down. I ached all over. Even my jaws hurt from biting down so hard. I was so very tired I rolled over and laid my cheek against the cool brick and drifted back to sleep.

In my dream I heard myself crying, weeping for the lost baby. But then I woke up again, and I could still hear the faint, faraway crying, high and thin, like metal scraping against metal. I got myself to my feet. Hanging on to the stone wall and the stair rail, I worked my way up towards the sound. My dress was stiff and stuck to the back of my legs. At the top of the stairs, I stopped and leaned against the door frame. The kerosene lamp burned bright in the middle of the kitchen table. Karl had lifted a black iron lid and was feeding cobs into the cookstove. I could feel the warmth clear across the room. I pulled a chair out from the table and dropped down into it and folded my hands in my new lap.

Karl turned around and waved his hand, beckoning me to him, but I couldn't move. "Come here, girl," he said, pulling me up with his voice.

When I got around the table to him, he reached over and opened the door of the warming oven up at the back of the stove. Inside, wrapped in a towel, was what looked like a little red animal, a new-farrowed piglet maybe. It took me a minute to figure out this was a baby—tiny but alive.

———

I sat sipping a bitter cup of heated up coffee and looking out the kitchen window. The rain had let up, and the clouds were drifting away. The barnyard was littered with hailstones the size of bird's eggs. I'd tried to talk to Gerta about the baby, to get her to tell me what to do with it. But she just turned her back on me.

While I was still asleep in the cellar, Karl had found Gerta, bruised and mad but otherwise fine. She'd rolled over and fell onto the floor and worked her way with her elbows back underneath her bed for protection. I don't believe she ever in her life forgave Karl or me for going to the cellar without her. She'd bring it up every now and then when she was put out with me. It didn't seem to matter I'd tried to get Karl to carry her down with us. Far as she was concerned, we were both guilty of deserting her. "I promise I'll never go off and leave you like that again," I told her the next day. Without a word, she reached over and picked up her Bible and held it out to me. I put my right hand on top of it. "I swear I won't." But it'd be weeks before she'd talk to me again.

I was still a little shaky, but I put down my coffee cup and opened the back door and went out onto the stoop. The air was cool and rinsed clean. Though it was a summer's evening, the hail, to my surprise, didn't melt right away. It'd turned glassy and reflected the sunset sky, orange and gold and pink. It was like a gift, God's way of saying He was sorry for all the trouble the tornado had caused.

The barn tilted towards the north a bit more than before but was still standing. A few more shingles were gone from its roof. Karl went out to check on the livestock and reported back. Old Maude and Jenny, the cow, had been in the pasture beyond the barn and were munching away at the wet grass between the hailstones. But the windows in the henhouse were broke out, and all but about a dozen of my chickens were dead, killed by flying glass or hailstones or smothered by bunching up in the corners. This must've been happening just when I was thinking about them from down in the safety of the cellar. All my fretting couldn't save them, and I felt bad about that.

Karl was more concerned about what the loss of the laying hens would mean to him—no more eggs for him to deliver to the creamery in Mount Olivet and no more money coming in till harvest, and none then if the crops had been ruined by the hail. He planned to walk the fields in the morning. "Ve'll see," he said. His face was dark with worry.

In the unhappy twilight, Karl walked out around the house to see up close what the storm had done to it. The wind had ripped the double chimney away from the south side and tumbled it like a brick mountain range across the weedy yard. The southwest corner of the house—porch, walls, roof, and all—was missing. When I saw it later, I thought it looked like a fairy tale giant had took a great big bite out of it. And all the windows on the front and the south side of the house was broke out. Folks coming along the county road now wouldn't recognize the house was once Mr. Cyrus Morton's grand mansion. All they'd see was a weather-grayed old wreck.

Karl went up the back stairs. Glass and water and hailstones covered the floors in his bedroom and our folks'. "Verever I step in there," he said, "the floor vould shake."

He decided the upstairs wasn't safe for us to use anymore. So he fetched down his bed and mine and our few clothes. He set himself up in what was supposed to be the dining room way back when the house was built. The double doors on one side of the front hall had been nailed shut for all the time I could remember. Karl shouldered them open. The floor was muddy with melting hail and shattered windows. The wallpaper—roses maybe—had faded away, and the corners were thick with dusty spider webs. So was the fancy candle holder hanging down from the middle of the ceiling. I just stood at the door and stared up at it—pieces of glass like icicles and diamonds. Karl kicked at the mess on the floor. "You clean this up tomorrow," Karl said. "Right now I vant to board the broke vindows up in case it rains more in the night."

Karl set my bed up in the pantry off the kitchen. That suited me just fine. On the shelves along the walls were sacks of flour and sugar, boxes of salt and soda and cornstarch, tins of baking powder and such, lamp chimneys, a bunch of yellowing wax candles tied with twine, some jars of preserves and pickles, a big jug of laundry bluing, and Mutti's good china dishes covered with tea towels. The narrow room with its little high-up window smelled good from vanilla extract and cinnamon sticks and ground allspice. Over in the far corner underneath the shelves stood the washbasket lined with folded flannel sheets for the baby to sleep in.

Karl gave it his own middle name, Frederick. Somehow, during the tornado, it had gone from being my baby to being his, though I still had to feed and take care of it. When I nursed the baby, I felt like it was sucking all the strength right out of me. And something must've been wrong with my milk. Right from the first, Frederick was colicky and bawled for long spells every afternoon and sometimes into the night. All I knew how to do was walk up and down the front hall with the baby in my arms and beg it to please, please stop crying and go to sleep. Sometimes I cried right along with it. Karl would come in the house and find the cookstove cold and nothing on the table and yell at me to fix his supper, and the baby would commence bawling again.

I didn't hate the little thing. It was just that I was scared I'd hurt it or, strange to tell, it would hurt me. I was just a girl. What did I know about tending a baby without Mutti or anybody to show me how? Gerta was no help. She acted most of the time like a big baby herself.

I came to hate myself cause I wasn't a good mother, the kind that never gets tired and never runs out of patience or tender feelings towards her baby. It didn't even seem like my baby, more like a young animal—a runty pup or abandoned calf—Karl'd brought into the house for me to raise.

Over the next year, I built up my flock again with black-and-white-barred Plymouth Rocks. Jenny died. Karl got a sweet-faced Jersey at the county fair, and I named her Lily. I put in a big garden in the spring and all summer canned what we didn't eat fresh.

Once the baby was weaned, Karl went upstairs to fetch down our folks' high double bed from their shattered room. He was thinking he'd have it for himself and put Frederick in his old bed. But it was more than a year since the tornado, and the bed had collapsed, and the mattress was soaked and moldy. So he drove the wagon into town and went to Gimble's Used Furniture and bought Frederick a narrow brown metal cot for his own. Karl took Frederick out of my bed and into the dining room to live with him and taught the boy to call me Hannah.

Long before he could talk, Frederick figured out how to get his own way. He'd plant his little feet and fist his hands and scream till his face turned red as a cock's comb. If Karl heard him, he'd come running and accuse me of mistreating the boy and threaten to cuff me for good measure. I could see Frederick taking this all in with the sly smile of the devil's own imp on his face. Nights, I escaped into my old dream of flying away on the schoolyard swing.

Like Mutti, I made do and didn't complain. It wouldn't have done any good anyway. Karl, by the will of God, was now head of the family, like Vater before him, and what he said was how it was. And most of the time I was too tired to care. Over the years, I tended Frederick the same way I tended Gerta, the best I could. But, God forgive me, I never could get myself to like him. Even when he was a youngster, he just seemed like a littler, louder, more bad-tempered version of Vater and Karl.

Chapter 13

1941-1949

When the war came, World War II, all the young men got called into the army. Since he was past thirty, Karl was skipped in the first round, and then the Mount Olivet draft board declared him vital to the war effort so he could keep on farming. He leased Mrs. Winona Rainey's fields and worked them too. Paying it off like rent, he bought her late husband's old tractor, since Maude was too blind and feeble now to pull a plow. By the time the war ended, he owned all of Mrs. Rainey's place, a new tractor, and a good used Ford pickup truck.

Early in those war years, Karl commenced thinking just the way Vater had, that folks hated us cause of our German name. Karl wouldn't allow anybody on the farm but family and went into town only if he had to. When he came back, he always ranted that everybody there was whispering about us behind his back, that they were trying to figure out how to take the farm away from us and send

132

us to a prison camp for spies. "They're jealous of us, that's vot it boils down to," he said.

There was good money to be made in those years, I guess. I never saw any of it. Though electricity had long since come down the county road on high poles and black wires, Karl said no, we didn't need such foolishness, just like Vater. The same with the telephone.

Mornings, a yellow bus came along the county road and took Frederick to school in Mount Olivet. He helped Karl afterwards and during the summers. When he was a youngster, to please Karl he could be a hard worker, and he'd finish his chores just like he was supposed to. But then sometimes he'd have one of his temper fits and sass me, saying, "I won't and you can't make me," and wouldn't do a thing. Once, when he was seven or eight and I had my hands full in the kitchen, canning sweet corn, I asked him to go out to the henhouse and see if he could find any eggs in the nest boxes. He went out nice as you please and didn't come back and didn't come back. So when I'd got a batch of jars processing, I went out and found him pitching rocks at my hens. He'd bloodied two of them by the time I got there and stopped him. You couldn't tell when he'd change on you just like that.

One thing for sure, he'd never much liked the every-night Bible readings after supper. When he was about ten, he figured out if he waited till Karl fell asleep in Vater's old Morris chair, he could get up from his place across from me at the center table and leave. He acted like I wasn't even there.

Once Frederick got to high school, he gave Karl real trouble, just like Karl had done to Vater. The boy had grown into a stocky young fellow with dark hair falling across his forehead. He was clean-shaved but had the furious black eyebrows of all the Meier men. He'd turned into a glib talker that knew how to get around doing his work by making it look like he was already busy. And Karl was always getting stuck with something he'd thought Frederick had done before he left. What with tractors and such, boys in the country learn to drive at thirteen and fourteen. Karl wouldn't let Frederick take the pickup truck, though. So, he took off with his friends whenever they'd come by in their fathers' automobiles. Karl's anger would be all used up in banging around the house and hollering at Gerta and me before Frederick came sneaking back in late at night.

I could watch all this, since it wasn't any of my concern. To this day, what Frederick thinks and why he does what he does is pure mystery to me. I've always been just somebody to do for him, cooking and washing and such. Karl's the one he's cared enough about to talk to and argue with and bedevil.

Frederick wasn't much of a student, but he kept on going in to Mount Olivet High School—mostly, it seemed to me, for the company of the other fellows and the pranks he could pull off with them. Karl laughed and egged him on, telling him stories of his own schoolboy troublemaking. He only lost patience when the joke was on him—like when Frederick uprooted the scarecrow from my garden and propped it up, leaning over the engine of the pickup, and went off to town with a bunch of fellows instead of changing the spark plugs the way he was supposed to.

I kept hoping he'd carry home books from school once in a while and I'd get to read them late at night while everybody else was asleep. But Frederick never brought home any schoolwork of any kind. Somehow, he scraped by on fast talk and what he could manage to get done, I suppose, during school hours. Anyway, in 1949, when school let out for the summer and Frederick was coming up on sixteen, old enough to quit according to the law, he said, "I'm never going back, and you can't make me." That was that.

The old broom factory in Mount Olivet had burned to the ground about five years before, with a glow you could see in the western night sky, like the sun had changed its mind and was coming back up again where it had set hours before. Now Mr. Vernon Lefler and some other folks had decided to rebuild it, and Frederick wanted to move to town and work construction. Karl shut the two of them up in their bedroom. I was in the kitchen, peeling potatoes for supper. I listened to them arguing but couldn't hardly make out the words.

Finally, I heard the door open, and Frederick came out, saying, "You'll see. I'm going to make lots of money, and by the time summer's half over, I'll have me a car, used maybe, but one with a good-running motor. No matter what you say, I'll get along just fine in town." His voice had sharpened steel in it. "It's not like you think. Nobody cares anymore about German names. If I stay here with you screwy people, I'll end up screwy too."

"Who you calling screwy?" Karl snapped back at him.

"You, old man, and those two goddamn crazy old ladies that live here."

I heard Karl's hand slap Frederick, hard. But it felt like Frederick had slapped me. I was going on thirty-two years old and his mother. To him, I just was a crazy old lady. I looked down at the hands in the cold water and potato peels—Mutti's hands, old lady's wrinkled hands. And I wondered, Do crazy folks know if they're crazy?

I didn't even look up when Frederick stomped through the kitchen. The back door slammed, and it was so quiet in the house I could hear the hurt forming like a lump in my throat.

We didn't see Frederick on the farm again till late in the summer. He hitchhiked back out from town with everything he owned in a brown paper sack with *Jansen's IGA Market* printed in red on the side—dirty clothes, mostly, he dumped out in front of me on the kitchen table, and a bunch of magazines with ladies on them without hardly a thing on. Those he shoved back in the sack. My face burned red hot. He just stood there, grinning, with a chewed wooden match in the corner of his mouth. "What's the matter, Hannah?" he said. "You never seen a naked lady?"

I grabbed up the dirty clothes and bundled them off to the washbasket, so I didn't hear all he had to tell Karl. The gist of it, though, was he hadn't been able to get in as many hours and make as much money as he'd figured working construction, so he quit. Or got fired, most likely. He made it sound like a joke that when he didn't pay his rent, his landlady called Sheriff Ed Garlin to throw him out. So he'd come home to the farm.

Like I told my chickens, I wasn't happy to see him back again, but I wasn't exactly unhappy either. "Karl's been so shorthanded and cross without him, I got to be glad here's some help come at last," I said and gave them another scoop of laying mash. An old hen named Mariah flapped down from her perch on the roost and crowded in with the rest around the feeder trough. She tilted her head and looked up at me a little doubtful. "I'll just tend to my own chores," I said, "and stay out of his way."

It turned out that wasn't very hard to do, since Frederick never had much to say to me besides ordering me around—"More coffee . . . darn this sock . . . why isn't supper ready?"—the way he'd grown up seeing Karl do.

Late one afternoon soon after Frederick got back, I was out in the garden, weeding and picking tomatoes and cucumbers for supper. At first, I figured it was just crows. But after a minute, I was sure I heard voices coming from across the pasture. Over on the other side of the rise, down by Turkey Creek, somebody was shouting and laughing out loud—several folks, it sounded like. I straightened up and rubbed my hands on my apron to wipe off the dirt and tried to figure out what was going on. Finally, my curiosity got the best of me. I unlatched the stock gate and took off walking towards the sounds.

In the shadow of the barn Bess, old Lily's daughter that was our milch cow in those days, lifted her fawn-colored head from where she was pulling at the short grass with her soft muzzle. Her tail switched at flies and her brown eyes followed me. She must've been surprised to see me when it wasn't milking time, picking my way across her pasture and trying not to step in any fresh cowpats. On the far side, I squeezed pairs of fence wires together and wiggled through between them and walked on, almost on tiptoes, towards the creek.

Close to the top of the rise, I got down on my hands and knees and crawled through the weeds. I wanted to see, but I didn't want anybody to see me. The voices were louder now. It was clear they belonged to several young men, and one of them, I recognized, was Frederick. When I got close enough, I stopped, flat on my belly, and lifted my head real slow. I could see there were five of them altogether. Like Frederick, they wore white cotton under-wear shirts—what he called T-shirts—and blue jeans. Since he commenced going to high school, he'd refused to wear bib overalls like Karl and Vater did. Frederick and the other fellows had pulled off their shoes and socks and were wading through the shallow water on the other side of Turkey Creek.

A big watermelon lay busted open on a flat outcrop of rock. Black seeds and pieces of bright red meat and green rind sat in puddles of pink juice. The fellows passed a big bottle back and forth and leaned their heads back and took drinks from it. "Hey, it's my turn," yelled a redhead with sunburned nose and ears. He grabbed for the bottle. Fred-erick snatched it away first and tilted it up to his mouth. When it was empty, he spun the bottle around over his head and heaved it high into the air. It hit the trunk of a cottonwood down the way and shattered. They all laughed like it was one great big joke. But I think they looked a little scared of him and his wildness too.

Then one of them, a thin boy with a short, bristly haircut, that was standing on a sandbar, let out a big whoop and peeled his T-shirt off over his head. He tossed it into the brush on the creek bank and undid his jeans and dropped them around his skinny white ankles and stepped out of them—homely but at the same time, strange to say, beautiful. The rest of the fellows undressed too, fast as they could. The late sun slanting across the fields painted their heads and shoulders and their backsides and bellies with gold. They moved into blue shadow down to the water. It wasn't like Frederick's naked ladies. I didn't feel any red-faced shame. I knew I should look away, but, God forgive me, I just couldn't.

At that moment, it came to me Frederick and his friends were about the same age Jake Coryell was that summer years back when he first came to the farm to buy eggs for his father's creamery. Back then, I'd been drawn to Jake and scared of what it was drew me, and I felt the same struggle now, watching those boys swimming and splashing each other.

Little streams of water ran off their flat bellies and down their legs. Where their jeans had covered them, they were pale and tender-looking, like water could bruise their skin or a stone on the creek bed could tear it open. I had never seen a man's naked body before. I hadn't imagined it would be so very bare and defenseless. Even the clutch of hair at the crotch, the beard of the male privates, was no protection. It made me all of a sudden sad—sad for the young men that could be hurt so easy if anybody wanted to. And sad for myself that I was a young girl made old before she had a chance to be a woman. Inside myself, the girl that waltzed in the attic and got kissed in the cellar is still who I truly am. Does that make me crazy?

I put my head down on my arms and took a deep breath and inhaled the dusty rankness of milkweed and the smell of my own body's sweat. There might just as well have been an angel with a flaming sword standing by the mailbox at the end of the drive. I was never going to get free of the farm and the family. No craziness of mine but what went on around me was what wore me down, I told myself, and, far as I could see, was always going to keep me there.

Chapter 14
1956

*T*he chairman of the Women's Division of the 1956 Wooten County Fair over at Bethany was Mrs. Vernon Lefler. She still came to the farm maybe once or twice a year and visited with Gerta, even though Karl'd send her away, just like Vater had, if he was around when her automobile turned into the drive. But this July morning, Karl and Frederick were out in the fields cultivating. I heard the sound of an auto pull up next to the back stoop and looked out the kitchen window to see her carroty curls pop up on the other side of the shiny blue roof. I poked up the fire under the pot on the cookstove so I could offer her a cup of coffee.

Mrs. Lefler rapped on the door and, without waiting, let herself in. She was wearing her usual half-circle smile. Over the years, she'd hardly changed at all, though I figured the color of her hair most likely got a little help these days from Ardith's Salon de Beauty. Mrs. Lefler still fa-

vored dresses printed with bright flowers, and she still had
the fullness and bounce of a gunnysack stuffed with rubber
balls. "Good morning, Hannah," she said, talking right
away. "How're you? My, it's been a while, hasn't it? I don't
believe I've been out this way since last spring." I raised
the coffee pot and offered to pour her a cup. She went right
on. "No, thanks. I only stopped for a quick visit with you
and Gerta today, and then I have to be off again. Lots of
stops to make yet before lunch."

I followed Mrs. Lefler through the front hall with a
kerosene lamp, but she seemed to carry her own sunshine
into Gerta's dusky room. My sister turned her head towards us and smiled for the first time in weeks. Over the
twenty-some years since the accident, she'd got large and
soft and pasty white. Her thinning hair had gone drab, and
her weight made her specially uncomfortable—and hard
to please—in the hot weather. I needed all my Christian
forbearance these times to take care of her. With company
there, I realized all of a sudden how ashamed Gerta must
feel about how she looked and how terrible it must've
been to be trapped in that bed, in that body, for the rest of
her life.

I pulled up the chair for Mrs. Lefler, and she sat
down, talking to Gerta a mile a minute, like she always did
every visit, about the twins, Bonny and Will, all grown up
and married now. And about Mr. Lefler's hardware store.
They'd done so well with the radios they'd been selling
since the 1940s, they were putting in a line of television
sets, even though the reception wasn't very good yet, but
Mr. Lefler and Mr. Harold Longstreet, that owned the
fancy furniture store in Mount Olivet, was planning to put
up a great high community antenna sometime in the next

year and charge folks so much a month to hook on to it and you could count on getting clear pictures from all the stations in the area, maybe from far away as the state capital. And on and on she went about the doings in town.

My mind drifted off into remembering the last time I'd been to Mount Olivet, the weekend of the automobile crash. Though I knew the names of some of the folks Mrs. Lefler was mentioning, I kept listening for one special one. Would that person recognize my name if he heard it today? Did he remember me?

My daydreaming was interrupted by Mrs. Lefler. "What do you think, Hannah?" she said and tugged at my elbow.

I blinked. "What?"

Mrs. Lefler laughed in her easy way. "I was saying to Gerta that I think you should enter some of your barred Rocks in the county fair next month. They look wonderful, from what I could see from the car, twice the size of most folks' chickens."

I looked down at the raw toes of my old shoes. I could never do such a thing, I thought, go to the county fair. But before I could say so, Mrs. Lefler went right on.

"Now look," she said, standing up and taking my hands in hers, so soft and smooth. Mine must've felt like sandpaper. "My job is to get as many women in the county to participate in the fair as I can. You'd be doing me a real favor if you'd do this." She waited just a second, and when I didn't answer, she said, "Good. I knew I could count on you," and smiled so broad her eyes almost got lost in the folds of her pink-rouged cheeks.

After Mrs. Lefler drove away, I commenced to panic. What had I agreed to do?

Mrs. Lefler backed through the kitchen door. Her arms were full of packages. "I know how difficult it is for someone as busy with farm chores as you are, Hannah, to get away to go shopping, so I brought you a few things to try on." Struck dumb, I put the lid back on the pot of beans I was fixing for supper and stood wiping my hands on the front of my apron. She dumped a paper sack and a big white box on the table and set to opening them.

I finally found my voice. "Mrs. Lefler . . ."

"Oh, Hannah," she said, shaking out a green-and-white striped cotton dress, "don't you think we've known each other long enough for you to call me Flora?"

"Flora?" I had trouble getting it out.

"That's more like it. Now let's see how you look in this." She held the dress up underneath my chin and leaned away to get a better view. "Good, just the right size." It was a very pretty dress, but why was she showing it to me? I couldn't get a word in edgewise. "You know, you haven't changed a bit," she went on, "still small as a young girl. How lucky you are. And the color's so good on you too."

"Mrs. Lef—— Flora." I stepped backwards. "What's this all about?" I said, waving my hand around.

She laid the dress down real careful across the oilcloth and smoothed out the gathers in the skirt. "Why, this is for you to wear to county fair next week. Remember? When I was here last month, you promised to show some of your hens? Please, Hannah, don't back out now. I'm counting on you." For a second, she looked worried, then she smiled again. "Now let me show you what else I brought." She pulled another box out of the paper sack and opened it and held out towards me a pair of sandal shoes, crisscrosses of green straps. "Try these on," she said.

I sat down on a kitchen chair. Quick, before she could see how dirty my feet were from the insides of my old shoes, I slipped them off and fastened on the new ones.

"I'm so glad they fit," Mrs. Lefler said. "I found them in the children's department at Mr. Perrault's."

I was confused and grateful, but too embarrassed to even say thank you. I stood up and stepped around the room like a youngster just learning to walk, staring down at my toes peeking through between the straps.

Mrs. Lefler laughed and clapped her hands like I'd done something amazing, instead of her.

First day of the fair, I was up before the sun and got my chores done. Without letting anybody know what I was up to, I caught four of my fattest, prettiest black-and-white barred Plymouth Rock hens—the ones I called Rachel, Rebecca, Ruth, and Rehoboth. I put them in a stout pasteboard box with holes poked in the top and hid it in the henhouse. I washed my hair under the pump in the barnyard and went back in to build up the fire in the cookstove and put the coffee pot on before Karl and Frederick came in for their breakfast. After they got up from the table, Frederick said something about picking up some fertilizer in town. "Ja, that's vot ve need," Karl said, and they looked at each other like naughty little boys and choked down a laugh. While I was doing up the dishes, they left in the pickup truck, headed down the county road towards town.

I washed myself from top to toes in the kitchen sink. I got the boxes down from the top shelf of the pantry and put on the new dress and shoes. The green stripes in the dress reminded me of something. But what? Spring grass? Daylily leaves? Christmas ribbon? Yes, that's it. Someplace, I still had the ribbon from the fruit basket Mrs. Lefler gave Gerta years back. I poked around the pantry shelves and found it wound around inside an old baking powder tin where I'd put it, clear over behind some Mason jars of snap beans and bread-and-butter pickles. I parted my hair in the middle and brushed it out, meaning to tie it back with the ribbon and twist it into a bun. But it was so long and thick it was still too damp. So I tied the ribbon around my head with a bow on top, just to hold the loose hair back.

When I told Gerta I was going, she puckered up to cry. "You'll be fine," I told her. "I got your lunch right here, and the chamber pot's there next to you in bed if you need it. I won't be gone but a few hours at the most." Her tears turned into sobs. "Please, Gerta, just this once." But she rolled over and turned her back on me.

Loading the hens into the trunk of Mrs. Lefler's Buick automobile, all of a sudden, I commenced shaking. For the first time, I was going off the farm and leaving Gerta alone. The picture of her face the day of the tornado came back to me—her mouth open wide, and her tongue curled pink and wet under her scream. And I remembered my promise on the Bible.

Mrs. Lefler slammed the trunk lid shut and got into

the auto. "Let's go, Hannah," she called out her open window.

I got in on the other side and folded my hands in my pretty green-and-white lap. I was feeling guilty and sad Gerta couldn't come too. But I was setting off on an adventure. Thirty-nine years old soon, and I felt like a young girl again with a green ribbon in my hair. It was a kind of miracle, like the raising of Lazarus from the dead.

———————

I set up my hens in the wire cage they'd marked for me in the Poultry Building. Such clucking and squawking sounded all around me and bounced off the whitewashed walls. I made sure my chickens had fresh water and clean straw. I put the paper sack of ground corn I'd brought for them next to their cage. Mrs. Lefler had promised me she'd see the hens got fed through the run of the fair. I told them, "You girls settle down now, or you'll get your feathers mussed. I'll be back for the judging at two o'clock."

And off I went towards the Domestic Science Pavilion to see the quilts and canned goods displays Mrs. Lefler had said I might enjoy. I never had Mutti's skill with a needle, so I couldn't make anything near so fine as the log cabin and Texas star and double wedding ring piecework I saw that day. And I marveled at how some women will take the time to arrange their string beans and whole baby beets in rows against the side of the Mason jar when they pack them for canning. My favorite exhibit was the part of the needlework section that had the rag dolls and stuffed toys made from sewing scraps—dogs and cats and little horses and even nursery rhyme pigs. I never had seen anything so cunning and clever in all my life.

When I figured it was about time to get back to my hens, I headed across the fairgrounds. Maybe I came out the wrong door of the Domestic Science Pavilion or the crowd of strangers rattled me a bit. Anyhow, I got lost. I worked my way between folks the best I could and tried to see what was going on around us at the same time. Mostly, I was just too short to see much but the folks right next to me. Pretty soon I could hear music, like a church organ, only with a liveliness that made me step along in time to the melody. Farther on, another sort of music came out of black boxes on a narrow stage raised up in front of a striped tent. I stopped by the side of the stage, back away from the pushing and shoving of the crowd. There, the sound was high and tinny and hurt my ears. Standing on tiptoes, I looked around and tried to get my bearings. A fellow in a flat straw hat was standing up above me. He was waving a cane and shouting something about Egypt and snakes and the secrets of the pharaohs. It was hard to make out his words over the whiny music coming out of the black box. The front of the tent opened, and a lady came out dressed in red and pink and orange robes you could see through, but not quite. She wiggled around to the music, holding a thin red scarf up across her nose and mouth. All you could see for sure was her eyes painted around with shiny silver and eyebrows drawn on with black pencil.

I wondered if this was what the Bible meant by lewdness. Vater would've called her the Whore of Babylon for sure. I knew I shouldn't be watching what this lady was doing, dipping and swaying inside her silky clothes. I

looked over across the front of the stage and saw the flat
faces of the men standing there. Their eyes gaped wide and
their mouths hung slack, and one man in a shaggy black
beard licked his lips, like this lady was something good to
eat. I recognized that beard. And standing next to Karl was
Frederick, with his eyes following every wave and wiggle
the lady made.

I turned and ran away between the tents. Just when I
was getting into the clear, I tripped over a rope strung to a
metal peg in the ground. I lay there in the dust, gasping to
get back the air that'd been knocked out of me and hot
with shame, for myself and for the Meier men, that showed
by the look on their faces they knew it was wicked to
watch that lady and went on watching her anyway.

––––––––––

By the time I found the Poultry Building again, the
judging was over and done with and all the folks had gone.
Hanging on the front of my hens' wire cage was a satiny
blue ribbon, ruffled all around a button printed with real
gold letters—FIRST PRIZE. I took each hen out, one at a time,
and hugged and petted her and said, "What a beautiful girl
you are." I refilled their water and gave them a big helping
of corn out of the paper sack.

Over and over, I kept saying, "This is my happiest
day ever." I wanted to tell somebody the good news. Mrs.
Lefler was supposed to meet me here to take me back to
the farm, but that wasn't till five o'clock. From the looks of
the sun streaming through the windows, that was still a
ways off. I felt so good I decided to go looking for her
anyway.

Across the way from the Poultry Building was the
Dairy Stock Barn. I stepped in through the open double
doors. I smelled the warm manure and dried alfalfa and
waited for my eyes to get used to the shadowy place. In
rows of straw-filled pens, dairy cows—fawn Jerseys and
Guernseys, like Lily—were chewing their cud and waiting
with the patience of fifty Jobs. They turned their dark
brown look towards me when I walked by.

I'd got almost through the barn when I saw a man
that I thought looked familiar. He was talking to a lady in a
pink polka-dot dress. My stomach did a somersault. It was
Jake. He'd got stockier, but not heavy or big-bellied like
some fellows. His eyes watching the lady's face were still
the same rainy gray blue I remembered. His hair was still
the color of corn silk, though it seemed to have lost some
of its curl and grew a bit farther back from his forehead
now. He nodded at something the polka-dot lady said and
smiled.

I'd heard he got married a long while back to Lila
Jordan, whose father owned the Rexall Drug Store. Her
back was to me. All I could see was her hair was cut short
and set in dark curls. She stepped forwards, and Jake bent
down and kissed her on her cheek. That was when I felt
my heart break down the middle like a cracked piece of
china.

After the lady left, Jake sat down on some bales of
straw over by an open side door. He leaned back and
lighted up a cigarette. In the slanting sunlight, I could see
him without him seeing me where I stood back in the
shadows. I tried to commit every detail of him to memory.
It had been, let's see, twenty-five years since that one gen-

tle almost-kiss in the cellar, and it might be twenty-five years or forever before I saw him again.

He was wearing jeans, faded but clean, and a red plaid short-sleeve shirt. His arms and face were light brown from the sun, but he was no farmer, you could see that. His tan didn't stop at his forehead from wearing a hat all day, indoors and out, and his hands, even from a distance, I could see, weren't scarred and knotted from heavy work. From Mrs. Lefler's visits, I knew he ran the Coryell dairy farm and, since his father's passing, the creamery and ice cream parlor too. He was most likely here to show some of his cows at the fair. They were probably too valuable to let anybody else do it.

I wondered if he knew Vater went to his grave saying Jake was the father of the baby that was Frederick. But how could Jake know any of that?

Jake got to his feet and stretched. He tossed his cigarette out through the door and onto the sunny ground and went over to a bale of alfalfa and pulled a flat bottle out from behind it. He unscrewed the lid and took a long swallow. He carried the bottle with him back to his seat by the door.

I must've looked like Lot's wife turned to a pillar of salt, standing there, staring. Here was the man that'd lived in a secret room in my memory since I was a girl, and any minute he could get up and leave again. I should've been shocked to see Jake drinking whiskey, but I wasn't. Somehow, it polished the shine of sinfulness already on these minutes of watching and wanting. Was I just going to let the way things are rule me like they always did, letting other folks decide—still letting Vater say—what I'd do and what I wouldn't? Or was I going to decide for myself, just once before it was too late?

Jake tipped up the bottle and drained it. Now he'll leave for sure, I thought, and pushed myself forwards, one shaky step at a time. I could feel the reflected heat of the afternoon sun on my face when I got to where he sat—or was I blushing?

"Hello, Jake," I said in a voice that came out too soft and high, like a little girl's.

He looked up at me, but his eye couldn't seem to focus. He put his hands on his knees and bent forwards and lifted his chin, straining up to get a better look. The empty bottle slid to the floor with a hollow thud.

His fair eyebrows moved up in that questioning way I remembered. "Hannah?" he said. I nodded. "Is that Hannah Meier?" Now he was half laughing. "God, you scared the shit out of me. I thought you were dead. Somebody said you were killed in a car wreck back in—what would it be, 'thirty-one or 'thirty-two?"

"No, I wasn't even hurt. It was Mr. Melvin Rasmussen that was killed, and my sister Gerta was crippled, but she's still alive, out on the farm."

He was still laughing, chuckling to himself like he still wasn't quite sure whether I was real or some sort of whiskey dream. Finally, he reached out and touched my arm, to see if I was truly there, I guess. His fingers went tight around my wrist, and he pulled me down to sit beside him on the bale of hay. His smile was wide and white like I remembered it, and the sweet smell on his breath made me dizzy—or maybe it was being so close to him. My hand took on a mind of its own and reached over and stroked his cheek. We sat there, looking at each other, till some fellows came in the far side of the barn and made a racket with watering pails and pitching straw into a pen.

"Come on," Jake said and took me by the hand.

I don't know what Mrs. Lefler must've thought when she came by the Poultry Building to pick me up at five o'clock. How I got back to the farm was Jake took me. But by then, it was the middle of the night. And by then, I'd had my first ride on a Ferris wheel, lifting up, up, up, over the merry-go-round and the other rides, over the tents and the fairground buildings, over the trees and the rooftops of Bethany. Jake had bought a whole strip of tickets. The seat we sat in swayed easy as Moses' cradle in the bulrushes while we went around and around and up and down. When the wheel stopped to let other folks on and off, we sat rocking high over the world, the lights below glittering like the starry sky turned upside down. I knew I was damned to Hell for eternity and this was most likely close as I was ever going to get to Heaven, so I never wanted the ride on the Ferris wheel to end.

And by then, by the time Jake turned into the drive from the county road and stopped to let me out by the back stoop, I'd committed adultery—not once but more times and more ways than I ever imagined could be—in the back seat of his gold-colored automobile while the crickets in the high weeds sang in jubilation.

Chapter 15

1956-1957

I waited for God to strike me dead. After a few weeks, I prayed He would. He never saw fit to do it, though. I guess He knew I didn't have the courage or the hardened heart to be a gold-star sinner, worthy of thunderbolts and sudden death. I had my shame for the sinning, it's true. I just never could come up with any pure regret. And He and me both knew I'd do it again if I ever had the chance.

Not that He didn't see fit to punish me. And the family did their share of punishing too. Though she was no worse for it, Gerta was specially bitter and hurtful towards me for going off and leaving her all those hours, and Karl was furious. "Who told you you could go und show those got-damn hens at the fair?" he hollered at me over his breakfast the next morning. He didn't even wait for an answer. "Mrs. Lefler don't run this family. You got no business leaving the farm mitout my say-so, you hear? Your place is here, in this house, and don't you ever forget it."

I'd had about all I could take so early in the morning, and winning that blue ribbon gave me the boost I needed to speak up. I turned away from the skillet of sputtering bacon I was tending on the cookstove, and I looked straight at my black-bearded brother. "And you got no business standing and gawking in public at a painted harlot just teasing up to take her clothes off."

Karl turned the color of a ripe tomato, and Frederick let out a whoop and smacked the oilcloth with his open hand and commenced laughing. "She got you there, Karl," he said and went on haw-hawing like a jackass.

Karl stood up so fast his chair tipped over backwards behind him, and Frederick's laughing dried up fast. But when Karl raised his arm like he was going to hit me, I didn't flinch or turn away. My hand with the three-tine fork stayed pointed right at him. I stared him down. He grumbled something and picked up the chair and sat down to finish his meal.

That blue satin ribbon with the gold letters was like a magic charm to give me a power I never had before. The rest of the week, I went about my chores, paying no mind to what the family said or did, and I didn't let their anger and bossiness get me down. The spell was broke, though, the day the fair ended. My beautiful prize hens got carried home to me in the back of the Lefler'sHardware delivery truck. With them came a note from Mrs. Lefler—she was so sorry about the mixup and missing me opening day and hoped I didn't have too much trouble getting back to the farm—but no blue ribbon. I asked the driver, one of the Staley boys from the size of the ears on him, to look again.

It was clear even from where I stood in the drive the truck was empty.

Without the ribbon, I lost my little bit of power and couldn't seem to stand up to the family anymore and speak my piece when I needed to. Late one night, somebody went into the henhouse and killed all my pretty blue-ribbon winners, beat their heads in with a big rock and laid them out in a row in the middle of the floor. I been killing chickens all my life, getting them ready for cooking. That was a sight that made me go outside and throw up. I thought for sure it was Frederick that did it. But I was scared to say so. And who would I tell?

Soon, though, I had a worse problem, only I didn't see it that way right then. At first, I felt a secret happiness when I didn't get my regular monthly. Every day, when there wasn't any bloody stain, I sat there in the outhouse for a few minutes with the door tied shut from the inside and smiled to myself while I pictured again the night at the county fair.

That night, I felt like I fell asleep and came awake in the Song of Solomon. There it says, "Let him kiss me with kisses of his mouth, for thy love is better than wine." Jake kissed me places that had never even been touched before. He stroked me like a kitten and said words so soft I couldn't hear them. I just felt them against my skin.

Our nakedness seemed natural as it must've been at first to Adam and Eve in the Garden. He lay beside me and took my breast in his hand and put it to his mouth, and I smoothed his corn-silk hair and whispered the sweet-nesses I'd saved up all those years just for him. I said so quiet I hardly moved my lips, "Behold, thou art fair, my love, behold, thou art fair." From deep inside me I heard

and felt the response, "My beloved is mine, and I am his
. . . I am my beloved's, and his desire is towards me."
Yes, towards *me*.

He said my name over and over into my ear, and
sweet shivers ran through me.

Though I blush to recollect it now, what I didn't
know, easy as you please, he showed me how. Like it says,
"I sat down under his shadow with great delight, and his
fruit was sweet to my taste." Biblical, yes. But I know most
of the pleasure came from the pure wickedness of it.

By the time he rolled over on top of me and the words
of Solomon's Song sounded once more down there inside
me, I was floating away, somehow, and he was just heavy
enough to hold me there with him.

It wasn't till later, when I sat in the privy remembering, I realized there hadn't been any pain, not like the time
with Karl. With Jake, what I felt was a warm and powerful
lightness that came back a little with each remembrance,
and, even now when I think on it or reread the Song of
Songs, it's never truly faded away.

———————

It was Mrs. Lefler that said what we all knew.

She came out to the farm with a Christmas fruitcake
for Gerta. Before she left, she stopped in the kitchen where
I was scraping carrots at the sink. I had on a big smock
apron, and I kept my back to Mrs. Lefler much as I could.
She walked up behind me and took me by the shoulders
and twisted me around to face her. "Why, Hannah," she
said with more hurt than shock or scorn, "you're preg-
nant."

I dropped my eyes.

Mrs. Lefler, who always had something to say, clamped her mouth tight shut. She stepped back and turned on her heel and went out the door. That was the last time she ever came to the farm.

This pregnancy wasn't easy. I was going on forty, and my body wasn't so elastic and forgiving as it was with Frederick. I'd sometimes throw up my meals, and I suffered from hobbling cramps in my legs and feet. Fetching water to the henhouse and bringing the milk up from the barn gave me backaches that kept me awake many a night. All this and the family could've beat my spirits down. Instead, I vowed to bear it with a smile—one that didn't show on my face—for the sake of our baby, Jake's and mine. The chickens just went on with their tails stuck up in the air and scratched and pecked at the dirt. Like I told them, I was finally going to have something to love that would love me back. That gave a secret joy to my days and nights.

The first two months of 1957 was one snowstorm after another. Often the roads were too drifted for anybody to get through. Several days might pass before the county road crew came by with their big yellow snowplow. I was glad to have gunnysacks full of potatoes and onions in the cellar and the shelves down there and in the pantry lined with Mason jars filled with the summer's peas and corn and tomatoes and such. Otherwise, we'd have gone hungry for sure.

Cause of the cold, I was scared for my hens. I wanted

to set up the old coal-oil brooder to warm the henhouse. But Karl growled, "No, girl, ve need it in the barn." Back in the fall, he'd bought some beef cattle in hopes of building up a feeder-calf operation. He didn't want to risk losing them or Rita, the new milch cow. So the chickens huddled together in one corner to keep warm, crushing and suffocating the ones underneath. A good part of my flock died. Karl made Frederick spade out a big hole on the south side of the barn, where the ground wasn't too frozen. I kept busy with Gerta in the front of the house so I wouldn't have to see the wheelbarrow pass back and forth across the barnyard. Frederick shoveled the stiff, feathered carcasses into the hole and dumped in a sack of quicklime before he covered it back up.

The hens that were left drooped around and weren't doing much in the way of laying. I tried to explain to them how bad I felt. I told them how sorry I was. "I did everything I could," I said. But they just looked away and turned their backs on me and scratched at the straw on the henhouse floor. They just wouldn't understand about the brooder. Or that no matter how much Meier blood I got in me and no matter how hard I try to stand up to him, Karl's bigger, stronger, and meaner than I'll ever be.

Far back as I could remember, Karl hated the cold like it was a person that'd wronged him on purpose. That winter, the anger towards his old enemy got stronger. He never stopped grumbling about it and cursing it. Someplace it says in the Bible to be careful about what you hate lest that's what you become. It was true. Karl's disposition got more sour and nasty and meaner than usual, and his black beard grew streaked with white, like dry snow blown into the furrows of a plowed field.

And at the same time my belly got bigger, Frederick got more hateful towards me. I could tell he was ashamed and disgusted by me and my condition, though he never told me so to my face. Fact is, he couldn't hardly stand to be around me and stopped talking to me at all. He'd sit at the supper table, forking in the food I'd cooked, and never even raise his eyes to me when I spoke to him. I'd be standing across from him with a cooking pot in my hand, and I'd say, "You want some more squash, Frederick?" And I'd have to guess from the way he moved his shaggy black head whether he did or not.

He'd walk in and out of the parlor while I read the Bible out loud in the evenings, picking his teeth with a wooden match and talking to Karl like I wasn't even there. Most of the time, he'd stretch out on the black horsehair couch and fall asleep and snore loud as a steam-driven thrashing machine. Sometimes, I suspected he was putting it on, play acting just to try to drown me out.

The cold spell finally broke, and late one night when I couldn't sleep, I got up and commenced walking around the dark house, trying to work the cramps out of my legs. I went around the kitchen table a few times and into the back parlor and around the center table and out again and finally into the front hall. I grabbed hold of the post at the bottom of the front stairway and leaned over to rub the back of my aching calf. The double doors to the old dining room where Karl and Frederick slept stood open a ways. I could hear their voices, and, Lord forgive me, I stopped to listen. The hall was chill and drafty, but that wasn't what made me shiver. They were talking about me.

"She's a disgrace to me and you and the family name. The whole goddamn town's going to be snickering at me, at all of us." That was Frederick. "If any of them come by and get a look at her, my buddies are going to start making dirty cracks and asking a lot of questions. What am I supposed to tell them?"

"Don't ask me. I don't know nothing." Karl sounded gruff, like he was ready to fight.

"Don't give me that know-nothing shit, old man. You know a whole lot more than you ever told me. Soon as she drops that kid, everybody's going to be talking about it, and I don't want to have to listen to them saying my mother's a tramp that fucked carnival trash and got knocked up. Naw, I ain't hanging around here."

"Remember vot happened last time you took off on your own?" Karl said.

"Yeah, well, I was just a dumb kid then. I know more how things work now. Spring comes, I'm going to get myself a job working on that big interstate highway they're putting through up by Lincoln. A fellow in Hoppy's Saturday night told me they'll be hiring and paying top wages. He gave me the name of the guy to see."

"You can't leave." Karl sounded scared. "I need you to help me vork the farm. Vot you vant from me to stay?"

"Naw, I can't live in this place anymore. I got to get out of this old, falling-down dump."

"All right. I buy you a house of your own, one of those trailer houses mit veels, und ve put it out back, away from the house. Vot you say to that?"

"With electricity and running water, indoor toilet, the works?" Frederick sounded like he was getting excited now.

"Ja, the vorks."

It was quiet for a minute. Frederick must've been thinking over Karl's offer.

"That don't change the fact my mother's going to have another bastard. It's bad enough she did it once and the guy ran off." That was the lie Karl had fed Frederick since he was a youngster. "Now everybody'll know what a slut she is. How the hell do you think that makes me look?"

How did he think that kind of talk made *me* look—and feel?

In the long, dark wait, I could hear Karl's hoarse breathing.

"She's not your mother."

"What?" The springs creaked like Frederick had sat up in bed.

"She's not your mother. Und you're no bastard." He paused. "Gerta is your mother."

I held my breath. What kind of terrible lies was Karl willing to tell now to keep Frederick from finding out the truth and leaving the farm—and him?

"Don't you say nothing to her, though. She's ashamed she couldn't raise you yourself." Karl was talking fast, making it all up as he went along. "Your father vas a lawyer named Melvin Rasmussen, vot was killed ven she got hurt. They vas married. It vas secret so's not to make your grandfather mad mit them. You don't pay any mind to vot your friends say. You're no bastard."

I was scared they'd hear me out there in the hall, my blood was pounding so hard, making thumping sounds in my ears.

"Now are you satisfied? Vill you stay here? Mit me?"

"Hannah's not my mother?" He sounded like he was

grinning in the dark. "I knew it. I knew all along that crazy old lady—reading her Bible and screwing trash and talking to her stupid chickens like they're people—I knew she couldn't be my mother."

So he was back to that again. It really made me sore. Here I was, I'm only sixteen years older than him, and maybe to him at twenty-three I seemed like an old lady. But crazy into the bargain? Why is it every time one of them looks at me and sees something they don't like they call me crazy? Well, if he was glad I wasn't his mother, I was just as glad he wasn't my son anymore.

"Vill you stay?" Karl was humbling himself, begging *his* son not to leave him. Couldn't Frederick hear that? "Vill you stay?" he asked again.

"Sure. I guess so."

Somebody, Karl most likely, let out a deep sigh.

"A trailer, huh? Yeah, I'll stay. But it's got to be new, and it's got to be way off away from the house."

Quiet as I could, I went back to my bed in the pantry. The sound of Frederick's voice followed along behind me, saying something about Karl trading in the rusted-out old Ford and buying a new pickup with a heater and a radio and on and on.

Frederick being so happy about not having me for a mother stung at the time. But truth was, for years feelings between Frederick and me had been like cutting off a dog's tail an inch at a time. Pretty soon, I felt a kind of relief that I didn't care, and that way it seemed like he couldn't hurt me anymore.

Chapter 16
1957-1960

There was never any question about me going into the new hospital in Mount Olivet. Early May, when it was my time, Karl drove out and got Madie Dakin, an old-time midwife from over by Elba City. The pains had commenced while I was frying the men's breakfast eggs and got stronger towards late afternoon, then stopped. Madie took a look and decided, "Might be false labor. Fix us some coffee. We'll see." So I got up and pumped some fresh water and put on the pot.

We sat across the kitchen table, talking. Madie was the most ancient-looking person I ever remember seeing. Her face was shriveled like an old potato left in the cellar too long. Everything about her was gray—her wore-out clothes, her wild hair, her skin, her pale eyes tucked into the deepest wrinkles. If she had any teeth, she didn't open her puckery mouth wide enough when she talked to let them show.

Dusk creeped into the corners of the room, and I lighted the kerosene lamp and set it on the table between us. It seemed nice in a way to have somebody to visit with like that, though I would've enjoyed it more if I hadn't got it into my head she wasn't there to see my baby delivered safe—but to make sure it didn't live. It was just that she looked so witchy and not very clean. While she told me stories about all the difficult births she'd attended over the years, I got more and more scared.

"They was the only twins I ever seen that come out one, two"—she snapped her bony fingers twice—"just like that. Too small," she said. She took a long, noisy slurp of her coffee. "Didn't last the night."

Notions about running away chased around inside my head like a flock of thunderstruck chickens. I couldn't make them settle down so I could figure something out. The men had got in the pickup truck and gone into Mount Olivet to get their supper at Hoppy's Tavern, but they'd be no help even if they was there. Gerta was down the hall and no use at all besides finding fault and saying, "You got yourself into this fix, Hannah. Now you get yourself out."

"Saw triples just the one time. Mother in labor for better part of two days." Madie chuckled. "They come out looking like skinned mice."

I was scared to ask if any of them lived. It might be a sign of what would happen to my own baby. For weeks it had been twisting around inside me, poking out arms and legs here and there, trying to find a way out. Now it had dropped lower and was heavy and quiet as stone. Madie held out her cup for more coffee, and I was just heaving myself up to get it when my water broke and flooded the chair and spilled onto the floor. I plopped back down.

"Babe's coming," Madie said with a wicked little giggle.

I sat and watched while she cleared the table and spread one of my clean bed sheets over the new oilcloth I'd got Karl to fetch from town. My belly felt like it was going to explode any minute. The pain wasn't like before with Frederick, not in waves but constant, like a tightening fist. Madie opened the gunnysack she'd brought with her and took out a brown medicine bottle. She poured some into one of the coffee cups from the sink and handed it to me. I could smell it was whiskey. When I hesitated, she took my wrist and pushed the cup to my lips. "Drink," she said. I never tasted anything like it before. It burned my mouth and throat like the fires of Hell, stinging all the way down. I wanted to cough, but I knew that would just make the pain in my belly worse, so I choked it back.

Madie stripped off my wet dress and tossed it onto the floor. I was shivering. My teeth rattled like sleet on a window pane. The old midwife boosted me up onto the table and laid me down flat on my back. She took the lighted lamp and shoved my bent knees apart with her elbows and held the light up between them. The glare hurt my eyes, so I shut them tight.

In the flashing dark behind my eyelids, I prayed to God to save my baby. "Let me die if I got to, but not my baby," I heard myself say out loud.

"Stop that foolishness," Madie ordered from what seemed like way far away.

The pain muddled my thinking and still clouds my recollection. "Wash your hands," I remember saying.

"No time for that," the old witch cackled.

I'd been ready for this baby for months, not like when Frederick was born. I'd made a crib out of the old wicker baby carriage without wheels I fetched up from the barn. I sewed up a mattress stuffed with clean chicken feathers and lined the crib with a rosebud-print feed sack. I got out all of Frederick's baby clothes and diapers. I mended and washed and hung them out all day in the sun to make them smell fresh and clean. I even took some scraps of print yard goods and made the baby a stuffed animal like I saw at the county fair. Only this one was a chicken, a fat hen with quilted wings and shoe button eyes and a blue calico strip like a ribbon around her neck. When I got to that part, I wondered again where the real county fair satin ribbon had got to. In my daydreams while I was sewing on things for his baby, I pictured Jake coming into the Poultry Building the morning after he drove me back to the farm and sneaking it off the cage and into his pocket for a keepsake of that first-prize, blue-ribbon August night.

When I woke up, it was dark outside the high-up window. I'd been put in my bed in the pantry. The house was dead quiet, and Madie Dakin was gone. A kerosene lamp turned way down low burned on the shelf by the door, and below it stood the wicker crib. I was scared to get up and look for fear it would be empty. When I couldn't stand it anymore, I rolled over and eased myself out of bed. The ache was worse than I remembered from the time before, and the pad between my legs made it hard for me to walk. I was shaking and wet with sweat by the time I got to the crib and looked in. There lay a perfect little human baby, its eyes squeezed shut and its hands fisted tight.

I wasn't past being scared. It was so still I was sure it wasn't alive. All I could do was lean against the door jamb and stare, till my knees threatened to fold up under me. I sat down on the end of my bed and tried to talk sense to myself. Here's what you got to do, I told myself, Touch it and pick it up and see. But I couldn't make myself do it.

I would have sat there like that all night, I suppose, if a soft cry, like a kitten's mew, hadn't come up out of the crib and set my breasts to throbbing. I lifted the baby up into my arms and sat back down on the bed. In the pale yellow light, I unwrapped the blanket and found I'd got myself a fine, healthy little boy.

Mutti'd had a brother named Paul that'd got killed in France in World War I. His photograph was stuck in the edge of the window frame by the kitchen sink—a thin young fellow in stiff trousers and buttoned-up jacket and soup-bowl helmet. Years back, when the two of us were sitting at the table, peeling potatoes or stringing beans or some such, Mutti would smile when she commenced talking about the boy she called Pauli and how he'd grown up to be so fine and brave and died for his country. More than forty years later, Paul's photograph was still there. Over time, the man in the brown-and-white picture faded to a creamy ghost, and the yellowed paper was curled up like a butterfly's cocoon. I decided to name my baby after him.

My Pauli grew into a chubby, curly-haired youngster that followed me around when I did my chores. He hugged his mother, he hugged Gerta, he hugged Karl, and Frederick too. He even hugged the chickens when he could grab hold of one. His smile was like the measles. Everybody that came close to him caught it. I don't believe there ever before was such a time when the family seemed to get along so well as during those first few years, all thanks to my sweet Pauli.

The summer he was two, he learned to help me gather eggs and work in the garden, though most of the time he was just mimicking what I did. I taught him to carry little gifts in for his Aunt Gerta—a pod of sweet new peas, a hollyhock blossom, a pigeon feather from the barn —and that way my sister and me got to be friends of a sort again. She asked instead of ordered when she wanted something. "Please, Hannah," she'd say, like she was teaching Pauli manners, "could you fetch me a glass of water?" She commenced coming out of her room for the first time in years, asking Frederick and Karl, one on each side, to carry her out to the table so she could eat supper with us. She still had to have the kitchen window shades pulled down, though, even if it was already dark outdoors.

Meals were about the only time I saw Frederick. He'd come in the house before supper to visit Gerta in her room, but he never stayed more than a few minutes, like it was something he was trying to get used to. He had no practice being a mother's loving son. Karl had seen to that. Sometimes he made such a show of it, I got the notion Frederick made up to Gerta just to spite me—and maybe cause of all the attention Pauli got from the rest of us. He was on his best behavior, but I knew Frederick's temper. His jealousy made me scared for my little boy.

Frederick was living now in his new trailer down by the windbreak. Such a commotion there'd been getting that big white metal box set up and electricity wires run to it from the poles along the county road. Karl had to have a new well dug for it and pipes run to a cesspool way down in the back pasture. I waited to be invited to come see his new place, but Frederick never said a thing. And I guess I was too proud to ask, though I admit I did a fair amount of hinting around. I surely did wonder what it looked like inside. Karl was down there most all the time too, it seemed like. The two of them spent their evenings together, except when Frederick took the pickup and went into town—to Hoppy's, I suppose.

Most nights after supper, it was just Pauli and Gerta and me for the Bible reading. So I moved the proceedings into Gerta's bedroom. When the dishes were all done up, I'd say, "Come on, sonny," and he'd take my hand, and we'd walk through the hallway together. While I sat in the chair close by the kerosene lamp and read the day's selection out loud, Gerta listened propped up in bed with her arm around Pauli. He curled up beside her, sucking his thumb and twisting a piece of his blond hair behind his ear with his other hand till he fell asleep. Like Sarah's Isaac, I told myself, here's the one that'll be a comfort in my old age.

It was a time of harmony on the farm, like I said. But under all of it ran strong feelings, like snakes waiting in the grass to strike out and bite you. Though Frederick had his trailer and did pretty much what he pleased after the day's work was done, he frowned most of the time I saw him and still wasn't speaking to me unless he had to. And Karl watched Pauli too close and made too much fuss over him. He bounced him too rough on his crossed knees and asked things like "Ven you going to come ride the tractor mit Karl und learn to be a farmer?" I didn't like that, and neither, it seemed to me, did Frederick.

Midday, I heard the back door slam and couldn't figure out who it might be. When they were working in the fields, planting soy beans like today, the men took their dinner with them in tin pails I fixed for them at breakfast. I was sitting on the end of my bed in the pantry. Even without a door, it was the only place I had the privacy to nurse my baby. Pauli was standing on the floor between my knees, wiggling and waiting to climb up onto my lap. I'd just finished unbuttoning the front of my dress.

Heavy footsteps crossed the kitchen, and I looked up to see Karl filling the doorway. His face was dark underneath the brim of his grimy felt hat, and the shirt behind the bib of his faded overalls was wet across the chest and under the arms. He gave off a stink of dust and sweat and anger. "Cover yourself, girl," he said, so loud Pauli broke out crying.

I pulled my baby towards me, shushing and trying to quiet him, and cuddled him against my exposed breast. He reached for the nipple and went to nursing.

"Stop that!" Karl yelled. Pauli pulled back and stared with his eyes wide. "You keep him a baby too long. He should be veaned a long time back. No more. You hear me?" Karl grabbed the boy by the wrist and set him on his

feet with his back to me. I clutched my dress front together.

Pauli was howling, "Mama, Mama, Mama!"

Karl raised his voice over the boy's. "Soon he'll be
three years old. He's got to find out vot it is to be a man,
not a mama's boy." Karl shoved his fists into his overall
pockets and walked to the door. He stopped and looked at
me over his shoulder and said, "The tractor's broke down.
Ve got to go to town for a part. Ven I get back, the boy's
things vill be moved already into the room mit me. He
von't sleep in your bed no more. He'll have Frederick's old
one. You understand vot I say?"

It was like being visited by Vater's ghost. My heart
was beating against my ribs like a trapped bird.

When I heard the back door slam shut, I pulled Pauli
towards me and settled him heavy on my lap and lifted out
my breast. His lips fastened around the hard brown nipple, and he commenced sucking, fast at first, like he was
scared he'd lose it again, then slower till his eyelids fell
shut and his fingers stopped twisting at his back curls. I
wiped the tears from his cheek with the hem of my apron
and kissed the top of his head over and over, whispering
all the sweetnesses I'd said to his father just that one time
and was sure I'd never get to say to either one of them ever
again.

Chapter 17

1960

I had to fight for my Pauli. I knew it was time he was weaned, but when Karl got back from Mount Olivet and went to move Pauli into his room, I told him no. Karl said he'd decide what was right for the boy. "You keep him a baby too long. I'll teach him everything vot he needs to be a man."

I was ironing one of the men's cotton work shirts. I put the flatiron I'd been using back on the cookstove and pick up the other, the hot one. "I'm not sure I want him to learn what you got to teach," I said, turning back towards Karl. "I want him to grow up and move to town and work at some job there." I meant for Pauli someday to escape the farm even if I couldn't.

Karl's eyebrows met in a dark scowl. "He don't leave. He stays here."

"How're you going to stop him from leaving?" I said. "Shoot a horse out from under him?"

We stood and glared at each other.

"Ach," he said and looked away. He moved towards the pantry, where Pauli was taking his nap in my bed, but I stepped in front of him. He was a head taller and, it seemed like, twice my size. I held the hot iron up between us.

"I don't want him sleeping in with you," I said. "You can set Frederick's old cot up out in the front hall, and Pauli can sleep there. And I don't' want you lying to him and teaching him to hate me like you did Frederick, you understand?"

"Nobody had to teach Frederick about hating," he said and worked his jaws like he was chewing tough meat.

He was right. Frederick was born with that black streak. Right now, though, I needed to settle this business about Pauli once and for all. "Suppose Frederick was to find out the man he thought was his uncle isn't his uncle at all, that all these years you been lying to him." I watched Karl's eyes to see was I pushing him too far. "You're such a good teacher. You taught him to scorn and shun fornicators and liars." I hefted the heavy flatiron and kept it up between us all the time I was quoting the Gospel according to Saint John, "Ye are of your father the devil, and the lusts of your father ye will do. He was a murderer from the beginning and abode not the truth, cause there is no truth in him. When he speaketh a lie, he speaketh of his own, for he is a liar and the father of it."

Karl looked like he wanted to grab the iron out of my hand and smash me in the face with it.

I didn't move, nor even blink my eyes. "You decide," I said and held my breath.

"I move the cot into the front hall, und the boy sleeps there," he said. "But only cause I say so."

I stepped back and let him pass.

Far back as I can remember, we had a calendar from Gettscheider's Feed Store, hanging over the cob basket by the cookstove. A new one showed up in the mailbox every December, and after the year was done, the old calendar's colored picture got nailed up in the outhouse till the place is a regular art show. My favorites are from the 1930s— Lilibet and Margaret Rose, the real-life princesses of England, and the Dionne quints, five little black-haired girls all born at the same time someplace up in Canada. Their pictures are still there, faded now, but I can make out their fine, happy faces and imagine their fine, happy lives. Though they'd all be grown-ups by now, I like to think they're youngsters always with their pretty ruffled dresses and perfect curls.

The 1960 calendar showed a picture of a fairy tale castle at a place called Disneyland, and that year Pauli's third birthday and Mother's Day fell on the same day, May 8. That seemed like a good reason to have a celebration, a family dinner like I recall from once on my birthday, way back when I was a young girl. Mutti baked a cake and put little, tiny candles on it, and I remember I got to make a wish and blow them out. It only happened that one time, but I'm sure it did happen. What stays with me to this day is the feeling of being blessed and in the Lord's grace that came from the glow of that cake. I wanted Pauli to have that same feeling. I wanted to make him a gift of that memory, since I didn't have a thing else I could give him.

All my baby's family would be there—except his father. I never let Jake know about Pauli for fear he'd have the right by law to come and take our son away from me. I knew Jake and Nila already had two boys. They didn't need mine too.

My head was busy with plans for the birthday dinner. I talked it all over with the chickens, since I wanted it to be a surprise for Pauli. "What do you think? Green beans boiled with bacon and vinegar? He likes that, and so do I." Some of the hens looked up at me but didn't say a thing. "A yellow cake," I said, refilling a water pan, "Mutti's six-egg recipe." My flock of Plymouth Rocks must've took offense at that, cause most of them scattered across the hen yard, clucking and flapping their useless wings. It's a good thing I didn't mention I was planning to fix fried chicken too.

"What about candles?" I said to a sassy little hen when she raised her head to swallow after taking a drink. I puzzled over that problem for a time while I cleaned out the dirty straw from underneath the roosts in the henhouse. I couldn't ask Karl to buy the little candles in town. He'd just call it foolishness. I couldn't ask Frederick. He acted all the time like he wouldn't spit on me if my dress was on fire. Besides, he'd most likely say something to Pauli and spoil the whole secret, just for spite.

"Who else is there?" I asked. An old hen named Delilah flapped up onto the roost and tilted her head and looked at me. "You're no help," I said and went out into the morning sunlight. I was fastening the gate hasp with a piece of wire when I caught sight of Mr. Willard Hagenbeck, the RFD man, coming along the county road in his automobile with the steering wheel on the wrong side so he could reach the mailboxes. On pure impulse, I set out running down the drive towards him.

Mr. Hagenbeck must've seen me coming, cause he waited at the end of the drive even though he didn't have a thing for us that day. The old mailbox leaned cattywise like it might lose its balance any time and fall out into the gravel road. Its little front door was missing, and the box was punctured with bullet holes—most likely some boy making mischief with a .22. Vater's black-painted name still showed through the rust on the side.

I was out of breath by the time I got to Mr. Hagenbeck's gray U.S. Government automobile. "Good morning." That was all I could think to say. I'd never talked to the RFD man before, and I was all of a sudden too shy to say what I wanted.

"Good morning, Miss Meier," he said, polite and smiling. He was a fellow close to Karl's age, but clean-shaved with a fresh haircut and not burned brown from working out of doors.

I was calmed by the way he said my name.

"Mr. Hagenbeck, could I ask a favor?" I saw his hands shift on the steering wheel and doubt narrow his eyes. "I'd like you to pick me up some of those little birthday cake candles in town. For my Pauli?"

The smile came back. "Oh, I see. A birthday party, huh? That's nice. Sure, just give me the money, and I'll drop them off tomorrow when I come by."

Money. I hadn't thought about that. I didn't have any money, never did have. All I had was chickens and eggs.

"How many eggs would that be?" I asked. "Would a dozen be enough?"

"Eggs? Oh, I see. Yes, sure," he said, smiling and nodding his head. "Let's say a dozen." He pulled away but stopped by the windbreak and leaned out the window. "What color?" he hollered.

"What?" I was so flustered I couldn't think what he meant.

"What color candles do you want?" he hollered again.

"Oh," I called to him, "blue, please. Blue."

I waved after him when he drove away, forgetting till I turned and walked back to the house to fret about Karl maybe seeing me and getting mad. By then, I was so happy about the candles I didn't care.

———

Like Mutti before me, I never sat down at the table to eat with the family. While they were having their meal, I'd stand back by the cookstove, ready to fill a bowl or plate or coffee cup. Later, when I cleared and washed up, I'd piece on whatever was left. But this day, I decided, would be special and different. I was going to set myself a place and put everything on the table and sit down and eat with the rest of them—just the way I remembered folks did at the Leflers' house.

Right after breakfast and chores, I commenced cooking and setting the table for the birthday dinner. This bright Sunday morning, Karl had Pauli with him down to Frederick's place, giving him his bath, and Gerta was in her darkened room, nodding over her Bible. The house wasn't just quiet, it was peaceful. I was calm as cream on milk and so filled with simple joy you would've thought it was my birthday instead of Pauli's.

And in a way it was. It was the third birthday of me being reborn a grown-up. And strong enough to not let myself get beat down. Pauli did that for me. I finally wasn't scared all the time of the men, specially Karl.

And it was more than a birthday. It was Mother's Day besides. Pauli had been carried off from my bed to sleep in the front hall alongside the front door Vater nailed shut before I was born. But I was still his mother. Nobody could stop that. Maybe, someday, God would soften his heart and I'd even be Frederick's mother again. Someday he'd know the truth and be glad of me and be a son to me like Pauli. That was my hope. I pictured some Mother's Day Frederick and Pauli would surprise me with a celebration, and Karl and Gerta would be there to share it. And Jake too. That was my daydream, my prayer, like a birthday candle wish, to have the family reconciled in His holy love.

The table was all set with Mutti's good china and a clean bed sheet for a tablecloth. I left the chicken cooking in the covered skillet and the potatoes and the beans boiling in pots on the stove and went to get Gerta cleaned up for dinner.

She was in a bad mood, feeling sorry for herself, whimpering about how nobody cared whether she lived or died, that sort of thing. These states come upon her sometimes, and I try not to listen too close lest I catch self-pity

from her. And then where would I be? I think she was
missing Pauli almost as much as I was, now that Karl had
him down at Frederick's so much of the time. We might've
been some comfort to each other if we could've broke
down and talked about it. But that wasn't the family's way.

I got out her prettiest smocked nightdress, a long-ago
gift from Mrs. Lefler, and helped Gerta put it on. I was
brushing out her long, gray-brown hair when the back
door opened with a bang, and a racket followed out in the
kitchen. I was worried the sound of Mutti's china breaking
was going to be next. But what I heard was Frederick
hollering loud as he could, "Happy Mother's Day!" I was
so rattled I dropped the hairbrush. I bent down real quick
to pick it up so Gerta wouldn't see the sudden tears. My
wish was coming true. My son had remembered me on
Mother's Day. I dabbed at my eyes with my apron and
stood up again.

Footsteps through the front hall and the next minute
Frederick was coming through the doorway, and he was
pushing a shiny new metal chair with big rubber-tired
wheels on the sides. Greta let out a squeal like a stepped-
on mouse and clapped her hands together.

"Here you are, Gerta," Frederick said, scooting the
chair up to the bedside so fast I had to jump out of the way
or get run over. "Now you can get yourself around all you
want." He was grinning so big his face must've hurt. Under his lids, he cut his dark eyes towards me, to be sure, I
suppose, I was taking all this in.

"Oh, Frederick." The whine was gone out of her
voice. "Where in the world did you get that?" She touched
her clasped hands to her lips and admired the chair with
her watery eyes.

"I was in town last week, and I just walked in and

ordered it at Longstreet's Furniture," he said, pig-proud of himself. "They had it sent down on the bus all the way from Lincoln." His hands were stuffed into the hip pockets of his jeans, and he rocked back and forth on his heels.

"Why, it must've cost you so much money."

"No big deal." He chuckled. "Fact is, it didn't cost me a cent. I put it on account."

"But don't you still have to pay for it?"

"I'm not worried. It's old man Longstreet that should worry. He's the one that's out the money." And they both laughed like it was a great big joke.

Gerta reached out her fat arms for him to get her into the chair. He had a minute of trouble skidding and lifting her from the bed, but I didn't move an eyelash to help. She settled herself in and turned to smile up at him. "This is what I've always prayed for, ever since the accident."

I wanted to say, What about the rolling chair I built for you years back? But right then, the two of them had forgot all about me standing there like a piece of furniture, feeling the fool, still holding Gerta's hairbrush in my hand. For just a tick, I wanted to hit him over the head with it. Maybe both of them.

Frederick leaned over Gerta, and she gave him a look like I'd only seen her give before to Mr. Rasmussen. Why, she was out-and-out flirting with him. She blinked her eyes and said in a sort of private whisper, "Thank you."

My chest felt empty as a barrel hoop.

I drained the boiled potatoes and set them back on the stove top to mash. I was glad I had so much to do to get dinner ready. "Work, for I am with you, saith the Lord of hosts." That's Haggai, or is it Habakkuk? I always get those two confused. And my mind wasn't working very straight right then. I was too busy chewing at myself. What ever possessed me to think Frederick could care two pins about me? Where did all those stupid daydream notions come from? All I knew for sure was I wasn't going to let anybody spoil Pauli's birthday dinner for him, or me. I was going to put on a cheery smile, no matter what. I pounded the masher up and down in the pot. I poured in a dollop of milk and dropped in a lump of butter and went back to taking out my upset on the potatoes.

I could hear Gerta and Frederick in the back parlor, talking, though I couldn't make out the words of what they were saying. Every once in a while, they'd laugh like there was a party going on already in there. That just made me bang the masher harder against the pot.

My baby's surprise birthday cake, all frosted white and perfect, sat on a shelf in the pantry. The family would be coming in to dinner soon, so I went to stick the three little blue candles on the top of the cake. I was standing there, admiring my handiwork, when Frederick came out from the back parlor to the kitchen and pulled down all the window shades. He went back to the parlor, then wheeled by the pantry door with Gerta grinning in her new chair. I wiped my hands on my apron and smoothed back my loose hair and tucked it into its bun and was just about to tell Frederick to go call Karl and Pauli to dinner when I heard the two of them coming in the back door.

The only chance I got anymore to touch my baby since Karl took him from my bed was when I washed his face at the kitchen sink in the mornings and brushed his hair. My Pauli with his blond curls that never had been cut looked like one of God's own angels. But when I stepped out of the pantry and caught sight of him, I went stiff as a broom handle.

"Surprise, Mama," he chirped like a happy little songbird.

The long golden curls were gone, and his hair was chopped short, some patches clear to the scalp. Karl stood beside him in his overalls and hat, like a dark giant with a pair of shears in his hand. "You're a big boy now," he said from deep in his whiskers. "Remember vot I tell you? Vot do you say?"

Pauli looked up at his uncle and nodded. His rain-blue eyes turned back to me, and he said, "Surprise, Hannah."

Chapter 18

1987

*T*hey eat chicken shit and ask for more. I stand back by the cookstove and wipe the sweat off my forehead with my apron. It's hot as Shadrach's shoes in this kitchen with the windows shut and the shades pulled down to suit Gerta. Or maybe it's just me, waiting for this wicked bunch of sinners to turn peak-ed and get sick.

Karl's rolled up the sleeves of his faded red flannel shirt, showing his stringy wrists and the gray cuffs of the union suit he wears year round. His old felt hat he wears indoors and out he's left off cause his white hair needs trimming. I'm supposed to do it soon as I'm done with the dishes. Maybe I'll take the scissors and chop it off clear to the scalp the way he did Pauli that time. It'd serve him right. He's shoveling dumplings into his hairy old face, noisy, sopping up the broth of the banty rooster with a crust of bread. Maybe it's going to take longer to get to them than I figured.

Recent years, Gerta's mind wanders at times, and her eyesight's commencing to fail. She's still a good eater, though, got as good an appetite as ever. I never watched so close how she eats—takes her knife and fork and cuts everything up into little bitty pieces, like she was going to feed a youngster, then works up a heaping scoop with a tablespoon. She carries it up to her red lipsticky mouth that's like it was cut open with a knife. Very careful, she leans forwards in her wheelchair and doesn't spill a drop on the broad white bosom of nightdress.

There's grime and tractor grease smears across the chest of Pauli's T-shirt. His hands and forearms are burned brown from working in the fields, and he doesn't always wear a hat like Karl, so his face's brown too. The sun turns his eyebrows the color of dandelion fluff. He handles a spoon and fork like they're tools for digging a well. From the way he acts, you'd think this supper's good as any I ever put in front of him before. He's the first to push his plate towards me for seconds. "More dumplings, sonny?" I say, nice and sweet as you please. I don't know where that jumped up from. I haven't called him sonny since he was a little boy.

Pauli blinks and looks at me with those blue eyes like he's just woke up out of some daydream. "Yeah, I guess so," he says.

I ladle a couple of dumplings and some broth floating with gray chunks of bowel onto his plate, plop it all right on top of the picked-clean chicken bones, and hand it back to him. He digs right in.

These miserable, gluttonous souls don't even mark

how it all tastes different or how tough and stringy the rooster meat is, though it truly must be. Frederick dumps salt all over his after one mouthful but goes on eating and talking about something else.

"You got to take that tape back to town tonight," he says, pointing his fork at Pauli, who doesn't even look up. "You hear me?"

He must mean that television VCR thing with the naked lady the men disgraced themselves watching last night. Anger boils up in me all over again, just remembering what I saw. If I could get my hands on it, I'd chuck that wicked tape right down the outhouse hole.

In the light from the kerosene lamp in the middle of the table, the curls on the top of Pauli's head shine like golden rings. He says, "You're going in to Hoppy's anyway. You take it."

Frederick doesn't like being talked back to. His tangledy black beard stops quivering from his chewing, and he looks pitchforks at Pauli. But Pauli's eyes are on his plate, so he doesn't see him. That's how he gets back at Frederick, who's bigger and meaner, by paying him no mind long as he can.

"I ain't going to Hoppy's tonight," Frederick says, chewing a mouthful at the same time, and goes on forking more supper off his plate.

Pauli looks up but doesn't say a thing.

Karl's the one to ask. "Ach, vot happened? You been their best customer. They shut down mitout you." He chuckles in his gray beard at his own feeble joke.

It's not funny to Frederick. All of a sudden, he swings his foot around and kicks the old man's chair back from the table. Karl's head jerks forwards and his glasses fall off into his dumplings. Then Frederick tosses back his head and lets out a laugh that sounds like a bull locked in the barn.

Karl's white hair's flopped forwards, covering his face. He sits there like he's too took by surprise and shame to speak. His rough-knuckle hand still holding the fork shakes with a palsied waggle.

I walk around the table and pick Karl's glasses up out of his plate to clean them off. Frederick grabs my arm hard, right where I twisted it this afternoon chasing the rooster. Before I can stop, I let out a little cry. "Leave go," I say, tears I can't help coming to my eyes. "That hurts."

"It's supposed to." Frederick snarls. "You stay out of this."

I look over at Pauli, hoping for some help. He's staring what's left of the pattern off the oilcloth.

Gerta nudges her empty plate across towards me and says to Frederick, "Are you going in to the tavern again tonight?" like she hasn't heard a thing that's been going on.

For some reason, this tickles Frederick, and he chuckles deep in his chest and takes his hand off me. I wipe off Karl's glasses on my apron quick and put them down in front of his plate. While Frederick's distracted, I lean my weight into Karl's chair and shove it back up to the table so he can get on with his supper.

Frederick puts down his fork. His chambray shirt's wrinkled and stained dark with sweat, getting too tight for him. The top button's missing, and the corner of the pocket's tore loose. He leans over towards Gerta. "Well," he says, "truth is I can't go back to Hoppy's, at least not for a while. Seems like they don't appreciate me there anymore.

I got into a little disagreement with a couple fellows a few nights ago, sort of lost my temper. Can you believe it?"

Gerta raises her brown-pencil eyebrows and pretends to look surprised, just the way he wants her to. She goes along with him whatever he does ever since he got her that fool wheelchair years back. It's like she's lost her eye for seeing him true and ear for hearing him clear these days, all for a few geegaws from the drugstore. "Picking on you, were they?" she says.

Frederick rears back and smacks his hands on his thighs and howls at that. "Not hardly, but I heard these guys across the room, a couple assholes over by the pool tables, mouthing off about something, and it pissed me off, so I let them know it, real fast. About the time a few noses was getting bloodied, Sheriff Keene comes roaring up with his siren going and gives me a choice of staying out of Hoppy's or going to jail."

The very idea. He should've got locked up, I say.

Frederick drains his coffee, thumps the thick white cup on the table, and looks up at me.

I know what he wants, more coffee. Tonight he's going to have to ask. I can wait just as long as he can. Longer.

He scoots around in his chair, facing towards Pauli. "The tape," he says, like a threat.

Pauli nods his head.

Sore as I am at Frederick, I'm getting more and more put out with Pauli too, just sitting there, taking every bless-ed thing Frederick does like it's *his* house and nobody else has got a say anymore. All the stuffing's been punched out of Pauli. I want him to fight back sometimes.

"Hannah," Frederick says real sharp.

I turn my back on him and shake down the ashes in the cookstove's firebox, making a great iron clatter like I can't hear him. I take the cherry pie I baked this morning out of the warming oven. He's not going to get any coffee from me till he asks for it. I'm fed up with his evil, bullying ways.

"Hannah," he growls like a dog, underneath his breath.

The hair on the back of my head prickles. I know he's looking at me with those eyes like slivers of glass. I know he's never going to ask. I know I'm not going to back down this time.

"Hannah." Its Karl's voice, tired and wheezy. "Frederick vill have another cup of coffee."

Why'd he have to stick his darn old nose in? This is between Frederick and me. I'm not going to turn around.

"Hannah?" Now it's Gerta speaking up. I picture her scalp through her thin white hair, turning red as the rouge on her cheeks. "Is there some coffee left?" she says. "I think Frederick could use a cup."

She sounds shaky, scared. Why doesn't Pauli say something? Still, I don't turn around.

"Never mind," Frederick says, way too loud. "I don't want any more. You'd get a better cup drinking the runoff from Verlan Bent's feedlot."

I keep on fussing with cutting the cherry pie. I wish now I'd put rat poison in it.

Chapter 19

1973

*M*ay 8, the very same day Pauli turned sixteen and the law said he could, he quit school, even though it was the middle of the week and the term still had part of a month to go. When he was a youngster, I taught him his letters and numbers, and I had hopes—I was always cursed with hope—I hoped Pauli would be the one to shine at school. But he just got by, with never a push nor a pat on the back from Karl and Frederick, and by that time it was their say-so that counted most for him, not mine.

From what I heard around the supper table in the days before his birthday, he was getting plenty of ragging from the men to stay home and help with the field work.

Karl had on his dirty brown felt hat. He raised his head up from over his plate and grumbled, "Ve got all the disking to do in the Rainey fields this veek."

"There's maybe half a mile of fence down on the far

190

side of the creek," Frederick said, forking fried potatoes
into his mouth. "The posts are rotted out, and the wire's
all rusted through." He made it sound like it was Pauli's
fault. In those days, Frederick was first letting his hair go
shaggy, and he'd just got his beard to where it looked like
burned grass. How much he was commencing to look like
Karl wasn't surprising to me, but it must've given some of
the folks in town a start, like the calendar had been turned
back on them. "The seed drill's got to be fixed too," he
said and pushed away his empty plate.

"You through?" I asked.

Frederick nodded without looking my way. He rocked
his chair back on two legs and aimed his narrowed eyes at
Pauli. "My bet is the only reason you keep going to school
is cause you got the hots for Mary Helen Carter." Frederick
and Karl laughed like that was some big smutty joke. Mary
Helen's father was Ralph Carter that ran the grain elevator
in Mount Olivet. That's all I knew about her.

Pauli didn't say a thing. His ears and his smooth face
went all sunburn red, clear up under his light curls.

My boy had a sweetheart. This was the first I'd heard
about it. I picked up the kettle off the stove and carried it
to the sink to pump some water to heat for the dishes. I
was glad for Pauli, and scared. I didn't have much left of
him to lose. This might be what would take the last of him
away.

Seeing Pauli's face red, Frederick must've known he'd
hit on something. His chair banged back down on four
legs. "You getting any?" He snorted.

Karl guffawed and waggled his head back and forth.
His face was lost underneath the brim of his hat.

Pauli's eyes were down on his empty plate. When I

reached across to pick it up, I could see his mouth creep-
ing wide in a sly smile.

Frederick saw it too, and his whole body shifted and
his temper with it. His fist came down hard, making the
knives and spoons jump. The salt shaker bumped over and
snowed across the oilcloth. The kerosene sloshed in the
lamp well and the light flickered. "You better not!" he
hollered. He sounded just like Vater. Storm clouds had
rolled right into the room.

I put the kettle on the stove and kept my hands busy
poking up the fire and adding more cobs.

Gerta sat plumped up in her wheelchair at the far end
of the table. For the first time during the meal, she spoke
up. "Why, Frederick, I think you're jealous," she said, trying, I guess, to tease the clouds away. It didn't work. He
looked at her like she'd stabbed him with the bread knife.

Here was Frederick near forty years old, rough and
quick to anger, big and dark and hairy as a bear, and no
woman would have him, I was sure, even with an all-
electric, running-water house trailer thrown in. That
must've been festering in him for a long time.

If anybody'd passed by just then and opened the door
and looked in, they would've seen the family around the
supper table with the lamp smoking and folks stiff and still
as the dead. And so quiet, you could hear the cob fire
dying in the cookstove.

———————

That was the year of the crows. So many and so bold,
we wouldn't have had any garden at all without gunfire. I
tried a new scarecrow first, built from tree limbs and rag-

gedy bits of old clothes. It surprised me every once in a while when I'd cross the barnyard and see it waving at me from down the way. I'd catch my breath and say to myself, Now who's that? But the noisy, greedy birds weren't so quick to be fooled, and on calm days when no breeze got the rags to moving, the crows settled down, like a black snow, to feast.

I complained to Karl, who liked fresh vegetables at his table, and he gave Frederick and Pauli the job of clearing the crows off for good. Their way was to pick up Vater's old .22 rifle from behind the kitchen door and take turns firing at the evil birds, laughing and counting the kill when they'd had about as much fun as they could stand for one outing. It was left to me to bury the dead.

An early summer Saturday after breakfast, Karl took the pickup into town, and Frederick and Pauli were changing the oil in the tractor. I washed my hair and was standing out by the pump, combing it dry in the warm sunshine. Vater had been gone for forty years, and we still didn't have a mirror in the house. But I could finger how my hair had thinned out, and I could see the gray coming into my long red-brown hair easy enough without one. The hand that worked the comb, the brown-spotted skin and wormy blue veins on the back, that was now for sure Mutti's hand. Sometimes I'd shut my eyes and run light fingertips over my face, trying to feel what wrinkles had got set there. I'd already lived five years past what Mutti did. Did I look like she did, worry dug deep across my forehead, squints at the corners of my eyes? It was wicked vanity to even care.

But I did care. Just the night before at supper, Frederick had been talking about meeting some fellow at the tavern. "He said he knew you, Karl." Frederick pointed at him with his knife. "He said he used to come out here to pick up eggs or something."

I leaned against the sink and kept my head down and bit my lip to keep from making any sound.

"Jake Coryell," Karl mumbled.

"Yeah, well, I never seen him in Hoppy's before. He was pretty drunk." Frederick chuckled and scraped his plate a couple of times. "His wife just died from cancer or something," he said, chewing a mouthful at the same time.

I couldn't stand to listen anymore. I wiped my hands on my apron and went into the pantry, like I was going to get something, but I sat down on my bed and tried to figure out why I was shivering so. For years, I'd listened to the men talk about folks in Mount Olivet, wondering if I might hear some word about Jake. Now what I heard rattled me. I never let myself daydream about him and me together, except to remember the night at the county fair. He wasn't married to Lila anymore. What if he came to the farm now? I'd want to hide in the hayloft again, or someplace else high up and out of sight, and watch him. I'd look at him slow and careful and fill up my eyes like empty buckets. But I wouldn't want him to see me, not in this old lady's skin.

I tied my damp hair back with a piece of twine. From down in the garden, I could hear the crows busy stealing their supper and bragging about it. I thought, Maybe I should get the .22 and try my hand at ridding the world of a few miserable black hearts. I'd never fired a gun, but how hard could it be? First, though, I had to visit the outhouse.

For a long while I sat inside, doing my duty. The

privy was warm and close. The smell's something farm
folks get used to till it goes so rank you got to dump a sack
of quicklime down the pit. When I was a little girl, I was
scared of that dark hole. I got it into my head it was the
doorway to Hell, and I imagined all manner of Satan's
imps waiting down there to grab my backside and torture
me when I sat down. I built up such a terror, I took to
peeing in my underdrawers rather than use the outhouse. I
seem to recall a session with Vater's belt cured me of that.

Up in the corner over the door, a fly had got itself
tangled in a web, and the more it wriggled and buzzed, the
worse it got stuck. Off to the side, the spider waited, knowing by nature when to scramble out and get its reward for
patience and hard work. That was a kind of parable, I
knew, but it didn't make me like spiders any better. Right
then my sympathy was with the fly.

My eyes dropped down to one of the old calendar
pictures nailed up around on the gray boards. I stared at
pine trees and a big mountain with snow on top, all reflected in a bright blue lake, till I was almost there. My
mind drifted to Pauli and Mary Helen Carter. What kept
on troubling me was how I didn't want to leave go of him.
That seemed like a sin to me, though I didn't have a clear
name for it.

Years back, I'd give up on any plans for myself. Mr.
and Mrs. Vernon Lefler were long since dead. There was
no place to go, nobody that'd take me in, and anyway I
couldn't leave Gerta. Every time I even thought about going, I saw her face like it was when Karl dragged me off to
the cellar in the tornado, and I couldn't do it.

When he was a youngster I always thought I wanted
Pauli to leave the farm and be free of the family, since I

knew I couldn't ever be. My escape would come from this life to another better one I earned through prayer and sacrifice and doing what I was put here to do. I *had* to believe that.

But now I figured if Pauli left that would mean he was leaving me too. And I didn't want him free of me. Wasn't that being selfish? Vater was right when he called me a willful, selfish girl, and the years hadn't changed that one bit. The longer Pauli went on seeing Mary Helen, even after he quit going to school, the more I chided myself. Why shouldn't my Pauli have a girl? Wasn't he owed a chance to have what his father and me did, maybe more? We'd only had a taste. He deserved the full meal—with whatever girl he picked and that picked him.

I came back to the picture of the blue lake when I heard their voices. Through a crack between the boards of the door, I watched Pauli and Frederick walking across the barnyard from the house. Frederick had the rifle in his hand, and the two of them were arguing, about what I couldn't make out. They passed beside the privy, both talking at once, and then stopped. I shifted around and found them again through a space between the boards of the back wall.

"Karl told me I got the pickup tonight," Pauli said. "Me and Mary Helen are going to the show over at Elba City. You can hitch a ride with me as far as Hoppy's."

"Listen to you, telling me you'll give *me* a ride. Who was it taught you to drive the goddamn pickup in the first place, back when you were just a little fart?" Frederick hefted the gun from his left to his right hand. "Second time in a week you're taking it. You're getting pretty serious

about that Carter girl, ain't you, boy?" Frederick make it
sound nasty.

"Don't call me boy," Pauli snapped. "I'm not a little
kid you can shove around anymore." It was true. Pauli was
almost big as Frederick, fairer and slighter, but just about
as tall. Pauli pushed his Pioneer Seed Corn cap back from
his forehead. Just then, he looked so much like his father
that first day Jake came for the eggs, it hurt to think of it.

"Take it easy. I'm just being family," Frederick said,
"trying to save you some trouble."

"What kind of trouble?" Pauli said, real slow.

Under the shadow of his black brows, Frederick's
eyes pinched almost shut. He looked about as helpful as
the Serpent in the Garden. "Are you thinking maybe you'll
marry Mary Helen Carter? I'll bet her old man don't even
know you two are still sneaking around, seeing each other.
You thinking someday he'll change his mind and let you
get married?"

Pauli looked down at the ground, working the toe of
his boot under a clump of dandelion, trying to root it out.
"Maybe." He looked up, straight at Frederick. "Why not, if
we want to?"

Frederick let out a laugh so loud the crows down in
the garden lifted into the air, cawing back echoes of his
scorn.

"There's nobody in this county that's going to let you
marry into their family. It's time you got that straight."

Pauli looked hard at him. "Why not?"

Why not? I asked myself too. It hadn't ever occurred
to me anybody whose last name wasn't Meier would want
to punish Pauli for my sin, and Jake's.

"Wake up, you little bastard. You don't buy that crap about 'daddy's with the angels in heaven,' do you?"

Pauli's hands balled into fists. He kept his mouth shut in a hard, straight line. Behind the men, I could see the crows were coming back, one by one, to light in the garden.

"What makes you think you're any different?" Pauli said, almost in a whisper. "Any better? Where's your daddy then?"

"I know my father, boy. He was married to my mother. And that makes a hell of a lot of difference, believe me. Nobody can call me a bastard." Frederick rocked back on his heels, swinging the gun down at his side. "Everybody but you knows your daddy was a freak in a traveling carnival show. Your crazy mama—holy Hannah —got herself laid at the Bethany fair, and nine months later you came bouncing into the world. They had to look you over real good to make sure you didn't have thirty-three toes or two heads or green skin like a lizard."

"You're lying!" Pauli yelled. The crows flew up again with a sound like running feet.

"I was there, remember? I was a grown man. I saw. And I listened to what Karl told me, just the way you better listen to me."

Lies, lies, and more lies. But to tell the truth about one thing would mean telling the truth about a whole string of other things, going back years and years. What would Pauli think of me when he found out how I got Frederick? That they aren't cousins at all but half brothers? What would Frederick do when he found out? Something deep in the space behind my eyes told me to stay quiet. To bide my time.

Karl would call me crazy. So would Frederick. And who in the world would believe me after all these years? What could I do against the lies if all of Wooten County took what Frederick was telling Pauli for gospel? In his face, I could read Pauli believed the lies too. A great pain ran straight through from my chest to my backbone. And I realized then heartache's more than just a word folks say.

Frederick moved closer to Pauli and smiled a wicked smile. "Never mind what those assholes in Mount Olivet think," he said. "We're family, and we got to stick together." He reached out his free hand towards Pauli's shoulder.

But Pauli ducked away. "Don't you ever touch me again," he snapped and spat on the ground in front of Frederick.

Frederick's face went dark as his beard. He made a frown like a fist and lifted the rifle and sighted down the barrel and pointed it at Pauli. Inside the privy, I opened my mouth to cry out, to stop Frederick, but nothing worked. My lungs didn't hold air, and my throat was stopped up, and no sound came out. I watched helpless as Hagar's babe.

But, God forgive me, how I wished that gun was in my hands.

Frederick turned then and raised the rifle up towards the empty blue sky and fired, over and over till all the shells was used up. The circling crows scattered, calling with a sound like rusty hinges and flapping off out of sight. When I looked down again, Pauli was gone.

Chapter 20

1987

I pray for another tornado. I know He promised fire next time, but I'd settle for a good stiff wind to break this poor excuse for a farm up into shreds and slivers and scatter it all over Wooten County. Some days a rage builds up in me till my hands and feet tingle and my breastbone aches. I have to get out of the house, or I think I'll explode and splatter my insides all over the kitchen walls. What comes to mind is the time Mutti was canning stewed tomatoes and a Mason jar exploded.

Whatever the weather when I get this way, I got to get out and keep moving. Indoors, the rooms are too dark and stuffy with black memories. Day and night, I hear the mice scrambling through the walls. Outdoors, I walk around the home place like I was on official survey duty, checking on the state of decay the house and outbuildings have got into.

My report for September 1987. Goldenrod and foxtail

and dusty weeds I can't even name grow waist-deep in the yard. Grasshoppers whirr and scatter when I walk through. Over in the far corner, the last of Mutti's daylilies bloom orange like bursts of sunset. Mr. Cyrus Morton's mansion, once so grand, now keeps standing more through habit than design. A century of winter and summer has turned the house's clapboards and shingles the gray of wood smoke, the color of its own ghost. The southwest corner of the house was ripped away more than fifty years back by the tornado that brought Frederick. The big double chimney crumbled to the ground, and the roof of the porch all across the front of the house fell down too, like the cover of a book slamming shut. Now the upstairs floor in Vater and Mutti's old bedroom slants and droops down over the dark front parlor that never got finished. Their bedroom wallpaper is rusty with water stains and peeled off in raggedy strips. Underneath is cracked plaster and broke-up lath. Weeds grow out of where their bed used to be. Woodbine and trumpet vine crawl all over their chest of drawers and dresser till you'd never know they're there and drip down over the edge of the floor like some sort of jungle in a geography book back in school.

Out behind the house, the barnyard's rutted and dry, rock-hard under the dust. The pen where Vater kept pigs holds a good crop of sunflowers and ragweed. A good half the wood shingles are gone from the barn roof, and the thing leans like a tired old man. It's empty now except for birds' nests and spiderwebs. Karl doesn't keep livestock anymore. He curses all government programs and refuses to let Mr. Merle Gordon, the county extension agent, even come up the drive. A few years back, Karl sold off the fields that was the old Rainey place to pay taxes, and Frederick went to work at the new broom factory that was built again after the fire. So he can have some money in his pocket, he said. Most likely to throw away at Hoppy's, I say. Karl and Pauli work what's left of Vater's land. Some years, to hear Karl grumble about it, they don't hardly make enough to pay for seed and fertilizer.

Karl runs his machinery—pickup and tractor and gang plow and the rest—year after year till whatever it is stalls, exhausted, and can't be patched together or fixed anymore. Then he goes into Mount Olivet or over to Bethany or Elba City and finds another used one to work to death. The pasture out beyond the barn where we used to keep a milch cow is scattered with skeletons of machines left to rust back into the ground.

I'm weary of what's left of this year's garden, a couple of hills of potatoes, some cabbages and squash, a few cucumbers still bearing, but the rest has gone to grubs and weeds tougher than I am. Myself, the body terrestrial Saint Paul wrote about to the Corinthians, on those days when I pace the yard, it sometimes longs to join the broke-down machinery out there in the pasture. It's anger keeps me going, though, and Pauli and my chickens.

My flock's just odds and ends now, small batches of chicks Karl's picked up for next to nothing at the hatchery in Elba City—Leghorns and Buff Orphingtons and Rhode Island Reds and even a few banties—and home-grown mixed breeds and culls we should've ate but that went on living year after year. I don't bother to name them anymore. According to Karl, we can't afford laying mash and oyster shell and such, so it's table scraps and eggshells and field corn I put through the old grinder. The hens give me a few puny eggs—and I do say, "Thank you, girls," before

I take them, for I *am* grateful—and we have chicken for supper once a week. I got a cellar lined with Mason jars full of fruit and vegetables and such, but these days Frederick and Pauli mostly like for me to fix what Frederick brings home in cans and bottles and plastic wrappers from the Jack and Jill Supermarket that took over Mr. Jansen's IGA in town.

The henhouse is patched and weathered, but it's still standing. The fence posts have got rotted, and I shut my chickens up in their house at night cause some skunk's found out how to push the rusty wire away and get inside the henyard. When it gets in during the day, that makes for a lot of squawking and wing flipping. "I'm coming," I yell at my panicky flock and go out there and hoot and holler and wave my broom and worry the skunk back out the way it came. I'm always careful, though, not to get close enough to let myself get sprayed. I hammer tin can lids over the weak spots in the fence, but it doesn't stop that polecat for long. We got ourselves a regular battle going here, and I'm not one to give up.

That darn Little David's the biggest menace to my chickens. He chases back and forth along the fence, barking and scaring them half to death. Last week, he dug under where I'd mended it and killed four hens just for pure spite before I could stop him.

Karl said, "Shows vot a good vatchdog he is."

"It shows nothing of the kind," I said. "It shows he's a stupid, mindless animal. He couldn't eat all he killed. He just did it out of meanness."

"Ach, Hannah, that's vot makes a good vatchdog."

"If he's such a good watchdog," I said back at him, "why doesn't he go after that pesky skunk?"

Karl bent over and patted the mongrel's head. The brim of his felt hat hid his eyeglasses. He went *ha-ha* way down in his gray-white beard. "He figures you make such a big show und racket at it, it's your job," he said and walked away, like that was the final word on the subject.

Karl says he got Little David for a watchdog to keep strangers off the farm, but I know better. Karl's taught him not to bark indoors, but when he's let out, that yellow feist yelps at everything that moves after dark and sets up such a fuss nobody can sleep through it. The truth is Karl got the pup to keep track of the fellows' comings and goings. Frederick goes into town nights, sometimes Pauli too, even after Karl's told them not to. Years back, he used to hide the keys to the pickup, but Pauli knew how to hot-wire it, like he said. And finally, Frederick got his own set of keys made at Lefler's Hardware. He pretty much comes and goes as he pleases now, Pauli with him when he feels like it. Little David out there yipping and yapping gives Karl a chance to get up and go out in his nightshirt and his ratty felt hat, leaning on that old cane, and yell bloody murder at the fellows when they come driving back in after midnight. I keep his bed in the front hall made up with clean sheets, but Pauli sleeps down at the trailer with Frederick most of the time so he won't have to listen to Karl and Little David carry on.

The white paint on the trailer's turned to streaky chalk, and the tar paper Frederick put on to stop the roof from leaking is curling up at the edges. I still haven't been inside the place. But I don't care. Most likely it stinks in there by now, considering what kind of housekeepers the men are. I sometimes go down and look through the trailer window when Karl and Frederick and Pauli are watching the television. Even by the little bit of colored, flickering light, I can see it's a mess in there—beer cans and bottles and clothes everywhere—and I'll be damned to burn in Hell for eternity before I'd ask to be invited in just so they can turn around and make me to clean up their filth.

––––––––

Gerta's got a collection of hurts and made-up grievances she recites every evening while I read out loud from the Bible. These days, to make out the words I have to use the magnifying glass Frederick got for Gerta when her eyesight commenced failing.

Tonight, we're in her room, and I'm reading from Psalms. "Let the sighing of the prisoner come before Thee."

And at the same time, Gerta's whining, "You were always jealous of me. That's why you keep me a prisoner, tied up in this bed."

"According to the greatness of the power, preserve Thou those that are appointed to die."

"I was always prettier than you ever were. And you're just waiting for me to die. But I'm not going to. Not ever."

"And render unto our neighbors sevenfold into their bosom their reproach, wherefore they have reproached Thee, O Lord." Now what do you suppose that means? It's like when I was a girl reading at the parlor table and looking to Mutti to explain. She wouldn't, or couldn't. Vater always made it sound like he knew what he was saying when he thundered out the Word. The old fraud. I know that trick. When I don't know what it means, I read it out anyway, good and loud.

Vater. He's on my mind tonight. That crooked old man that thought he was God—and I thought so too. But knowing what he was, saying it to myself, doesn't drive out all his power over me. He was right when he told me that time, "You cannot hide from your vater." Not even when he's dead fifty years and more.

"A wonderful man loves me, and he's coming back for me any day now," Gerta's saying. "Don't you keep him waiting. You let him in the minute he gets here. We're going in to Mount Olivet, and Judge Tatum is going to marry us."

It's always a job to see who's going to get tired and shut up first. This night, I read on till I don't hear her jabbering anymore. I look up, and Gerta's laying there with her white mouth open and the sound of her breath catching deep in her throat. Her thin hair is like a tangle of cobwebs. Her eyebrows are brown half circles she draws on, and her fat cheeks are blotched red with rouge, paint she gets Frederick to fetch her from town. He's good to Gerta, when he wants to be, but I wonder sometimes if maybe it's not just to spite me.

I finish my reading loud enough to drown out her snores. "So we people and sheep of Thy pasture will give Thee thanks forever." I'm quieter, almost done. "We will show forth Thy praise to all generations."

I lay the little red ribbon between the pages to mark the place and shut the Bible in my lap. My mind still holds the picture of Mutti and Vater in the parlor, and I hear him saying, "Honor thy vater und thy mutter," in his God-voice that used to scare the starch out of me. But now I think, Honor him? Why? What for? I feel more like cursing him, the mean old devil. And he taught Karl to be the same. I have these bad dreams about the night I got Frederick against my will, and it's Vater, not Karl, that's doing it to me. I wake up fighting with the covers and cursing him, using words I never spoke in the daylight.

"Whoso curseth father or mother," according to Saint Mark, "let him die the death." I open the Bible again and flip through the pages to find the rest of that passage. "But ye say, If a man shall say to his father or mother, It is Corban"—who is this fellow Corban? I wonder—"that is to say, a gift, by whatsoever thou mightest be profited by me, he shall be free." I want to be free, free of Vater and the echoes of Vater. Free of all the black memories where he still lives. But how can I do that if I don't understand any of what it says to do in my reading here? It just makes me mad.

I put the Bible and the magnifying glass down on the chair and turn out the kerosene lamp.

My feet and legs are tingly restless again tonight. I won't be able to sleep till I walk it off. Outdoors, the full moon comes and goes behind clouds like steel wool. Crickets are singing in the settling damp. In the drive, Karl's pickup stands on the shadow side of the house. I make a trip around the barnyard, and I'm still tied full of knots, so I set off down towards the windbreak and the trailer. I know all three of them are in there.

I'm thinking, I got through the years the best I could, not so holy I knew God's first name, but I tried to live by His Word, in spite of the trials He sent me. I never let hatred nibble away at my heart, though I was provoked often enough to have a right to it. Feeling sorry for yourself just makes matters worse, Mutti used to say, so I kept busy and didn't dwell on my hurts like Gerta does. I accepted whatever came, the way the Bible tells us to. Whether it's the fruit or the flower of the tree doesn't concern me. My reward will be in Heaven, I told myself. And I mostly believed it, but I'm wondering now if forbearance is such a wonderful great virtue after all. I'm seventy last week, just white hair and bones now, wearing a sagging union suit of freckled skin stretched too big for me. There's not much I'm scared of anymore, just a lot that makes me want to call Him to account for. I'm almost ready to die so I can face Him and make Him explain. I figure Judgment Day works both ways.

I haven't got a bless-ed thing in this life to lose, except for the sight of my Pauli. He's a grown man, easygoing, maybe too easygoing, too willing to go along with Karl and Frederick and not upset them—too much like me in that way. But I'll say this, he's a good man, patient with Karl's rantings and Gerta's foolishness. Maybe he gets drunk once in a while, but I blame Frederick for that, taking him to the tavern with him ever since Pauli got out of school. What else they do in town I don't know for sure. I don't want to know. I seen how drink makes Frederick loud and ugly and ready to pick a fight. Pauli's quieter. His eyes get all red-rimmed and sleepy, and his mouth curls up in a silly smile. Maybe he's not the loving son I wanted him to be—what that is in the particulars I'm not sure of anymore. Mostly, Pauli acts like I'm just there, like I'm the same thing as the stove or the kitchen table.

At least he never talks hateful about me like Frederick sometimes does. Like I heard him saying to Gerta the other week, the last time it rained, after I told him to wipe his muddy feet before he came into my kitchen, "Folks in town scare their kids with her instead of the bogeyman.

'Behave yourself or old witchy Hannah will come in the night and get you.' " I pretended like I didn't hear.

Pauli still looks the way I remember his father, with eyes like a baby kitten, big and gray blue and innocent. Back when I was a girl in school and Francie Matthews and Mabel Bent giggled about being sweet on a boy, I didn't know what they meant. I do now. For thirty years, I been sweet on my Pauli. That's how I love him, like he was Jake come back again to keep me happy, deep inside where nobody else can see. I'm just as selfish as Karl, telling so many lies to keep Frederick here. And Frederick, telling the lies that kept Pauli from going. I never spoke up against those lies. I might've told him who his father is, maybe even sent him to Jake when he was old enough, but I was sure I wouldn't see my boy again if I did. And he's the only one I ever cared about that didn't pass from me. Besides him and Jake, the best things in my life have been what I gave myself that I made up in my imagination, like waltzing in the attic, and I remember those things and they won't pass away till I do.

Not dying but surprise is what I dread the most. No more surprises, I pray every night. But God—or is it Satan? or are they both the same?—has decided to send me another jolt.

When I come up to the trailer, I look in the window like I always do to watch the television. But this time, I catch sight of a naked lady on the screen. I never saw anybody show off their nakedness like that, holding her bare breasts out with her hands and smiling a red, red smile. She wiggles all over. She winks her purple-painted eye. Most likely there's some kind of music playing, but I can't hear it. She prances around and squirms her bare pink backside the same as that dancer years back at the county fair. My cheeks are on fire, like I was slapped, and my eyes commence smarting with tears. But I can't look away.

And just like Susannah and the Elders, those three wicked men sit there, watching. I can make out their black head shapes from where I am. I can't see their faces, though. Dear Lord, why can't I just let it be? Instead, I work my way around to the window on the other side of the trailer and look in.

Strangers' faces. Eyes staring into the flickering light. I see it flashing on Karl's glasses under the brim of his hat. Deep in the blasphemous tangle of their beards, Karl and Frederick are grinning. I see my Pauli leering at her just like the others. The teeth between his lips shine wet like a hungry animal's. Is this what Pauli—and Jake too—is this what they all want? This wiggling wantonness? It hurts me to think so. Even at my age, it hurts. Is it envy I'm feeling? Is it guilt? All along, did I want to be a whore, like Vater said? Or behind all his accusing and punishing, is that truly what he—and the men, all of them—is that what they wanted me to be?

Lord God, you owe me an explanation!

I look away from their faces and see Pauli's hands folded in his lap, working sly and regular. I know what he's doing, though I don't have the word for it. I turn away lest I be struck blind. I wish I was struck blind. The sin of it. And the shame. I shut my stinging eyes, but the naked lady dances on the insides of my eyelids. I'm hot, flushed, weak in the knees, like I got a high fever. Dizzy and confused, I bump against the side of the trailer and stumble and run towards the shadows of the windbreak. Back there behind me, the trailer door opens. Little David is barking. I push my breathless old bones to run faster. Liars. Fornicators. Lusting after whores. I can't think. Just feel. Furious. Mortified. Outraged. Every step jabs my insides. Shamed. Hurt. Mad. I. Hate. Them. All.

Chapter 21

1987

*T*hey ate chicken shit and never knew. Now they sit around the kitchen table—Karl, Frederick, Pauli, and Gerta. Cherry juice pools and clots on their pie plates. I'm at the sink, my hands in hot water, washing dishes. I know "Vengeance is mine, saith the Lord," but tonight a little bit of it's mine too. I'd sort of hoped they'd get sick and be purely miserable for a while. For now, it's enough I know what I put over on this wicked bunch of unrepentant sinners. Listening to them talk like this was just the same as all the other hundreds— no, thousands—of suppers I ever cooked for them.

Frederick's sitting back and scratching at his chin through his wiry black beard like he does when his temper's running out. He's been telling about going to the courthouse in Mount Olivet this afternoon to try to get some government money for Karl now he's past seventy-five and almost too stove-up to work in the fields. To hear him tell it, we need the money, that's for sure. But Karl's stubborn mad and not being any help at all to Frederick.

"All they need is some proof of your age, and you'll be getting a check every month. You got to show them something, like a birth certificate."

Karl just sits there in his patched overalls and faded flannel shirt. His long hair falls forwards, hiding his face above his bristly gray-white beard.

Frederick's waiting. "Birth certificate?" he says again, like Karl's deaf.

Karl leans on his forearms, talking into his coffee cup. "Got none. Never had."

Frederick won't leave it go. "The lady in the office said years back they used to write down when everybody was born or married or died in the family Bible. That's proof. Where's the family Bible?"

Karl's folded eyeglasses stare back from in front of him on the table. "Buried mit Mutti in the front yard."

Frederick doesn't know about all that. "What're you talking about?" he says, real surprised.

Karl tilts his head towards the front of the house. "Over in the corner vere the orange daylilies gone vild."

"You mean your mother's buried out there?" Frederick looks like he just found out what he truly ate for supper. Pauli's eyes are darting back and forth between the two men, big as dinner plates.

"Ja. Vater too. He didn't vant no town cemetery."

Slouched down in her wheelchair, Gerta's listening to all this and nodding her head, like she's feeble-minded.

Frederick plants his feet hard on the floor and scrapes back his chair, but he doesn't stand up. His hairy-back hands are spread flat on the table. "Well, I ain't digging up a grave for no amount of money."

"I vouldn't let you, no matter vot," Karl shoots back.

"Never mind, old man. There's got to be something else around here that shows your age." Frederick's dark eyebrows pull together in a frown. "Jesus, don't anybody in this family keep any goddamn records?"

I'm trying to figure out what might be stored away yet upstairs that would help.

Frederick turns towards her and says, "Gerta, where do you keep your marriage license and my birth certificate? Maybe there's something put away with them that'll show Karl's age."

With all her working over the past, she may talk foolishness to herself at times, but Gerta doesn't lie when you ask her a question straight out. "There isn't any license," she says, so soft Frederick leans over towards her.

"What're you saying? You never got married?"

Tears are running down Gerta's fat rouged cheeks.

"Wait a minute. You mean to tell me you never married Mr. High-and-Mighty Lawyer Rasmussen?" He's talking way too loud now, making Gerta sob into her wadded-up handkerchief. "Are you saying I'm just as much a bastard as Paul here is?"

Something inside my head just goes snap, like a frayed piece of string breaking from the weight of too many lies over too many years. Brave or foolish, I see my chance and I take it, all the time knowing right down to my toes that once said, there's no taking any of it back. "Maybe it's time we got all that cleared up," I say. I wipe my hands on my apron so he can't see how much they're shaking. "Karl lied to you." I take a big drink of air to steady myself. I got to say it, no matter what. "Gerta's not your mother. I am."

"Wait a minute," he says. Frederick's face is burning behind his beard, and I can see he doesn't want to believe me. "Is that true?" he asks, turning on Karl. All of a sudden, Frederick tosses back his head and lets out a laugh like a wild man. "Listen to me, asking the one that's lied to me all my life if he lied!" He gets to his feet and steps around real thoughtful and grips the back of his chair, looking straight at me. "I guess I got to know the rest. If you're my mother, then who the hell's my father?"

Am I ready to say that truth? It will pain everybody in this old kitchen, every face painted with light from the kerosene lamp, everybody whose shadow's thrown up on the walls stained brown with years of cooking grease and smoky fires in the iron stove. I got the weapon now to hurt those folks that hurt me most. And the one that's hurt me least. Yes, Pauli's caused me pain, though not so much as some have. That's what's got hold of my tongue right now.

But anger's heating up in me too. Whatever happens, I got to stop going along with the lying. Let *him* take the blame that's been owing to him for so long. So I say, "You ready to tell him, Karl?"

What have I been scared of for so long? Dear Lord, look at him. He's just a shrunk-up old wreck.

Karl drops his head onto his arms folded on the table. Frederick looks at him and back at me.

Now he knows. Not just a bastard.

But it's Pauli whose pain-blue eyes I see questioning me. "Hannah?" And it's Pauli that says it, though it catches like a stone in his throat. "Karl?"

"Let me explain," I say to Pauli.

But before I can say a thing more, Frederick grabs
Karl by the back of the shirt and tries to pull him to his
feet. The faded red flannel rips away in Frederick's fist, and
the old man stays in his chair with his sinner's face hid in
his arms.

Frederick staggers back, glaring at me. All of Vater's
black wrath shines in his face. The old monster is in his
blood.

He stumbles out, leaves, slamming the door so hard
the rifle leaning in the corner slides down along the wall
till it lays flat on the floor, and the chimney of the kerosene
lamp rattles around a wavery flame. At the same time, out
on the back stoop, Little David's set up a minute's worth of
yapping, and the pickup truck roars away down the drive.

All's quiet for about two heartbeats. Pauli won't look
at me. "You listen to me," I say. "It's not how you think. It
wasn't my fault." He pushed back his chair and goes out
the back door and bangs it shut behind him.

White as a sack of flour, Gerta's asleep in her wheelchair, still at the kitchen table. She's cried all her rouge
and lipstick off into her handkerchief till it looks like a
bloody bandage she'd got clutched in the hand laying on
her flat bosom. It must be after ten o'clock. I don't want to
wake her up just yet. That'll mean arguing with her some
more and struggling by myself to get her out of the chair
and into bed. I look at her and try to figure out why I
stayed and took care of her all this time. Never a smile or a
thanks these last years. I knew my duty and I did it. Way
back, when I didn't know I had any choice, I chose to be

what Vater called a good Christian woman, like Mutti. Thinking about that, I feel the anger piling up in me again.

I been reading First Corinthians out loud, mostly for my own benefit. Gerta, wore out from tears, nodded off. And Karl, looking withered and pathetic, got up and left a while back. He didn't even put his hat on, just took his cane and hobbled out into the Indian summer night without a word, like he didn't have a bless-ed thing to atone for. What would it cost him, the worthless old reprobate, just once to say he's sorry?

I been trying to find some comfort in the Apostle's words—"God is faithful, Who will not suffer you to be tempted above that ye are able, but will with the temptation also make a way to escape, that ye may be able to bear it." I been sorely tempted to avenge myself tonight beyond bad chicken dumplings. My eyes keep wandering from the little black words on the page to the rifle by the door. I'm wore out from wrestling with my hate and anger, and looking for that promised escape. Saint Paul warned those Corinthians that folks are full of malice and wickedness, and I say amen to that. Tonight, I'm full to overflowing with it, the whole family is. It's like a sickness passed from generation to generation. Better it should stop, be stopped right here and now, I say.

But I read on to myself what Paul wrote about charity —what I take to be a special kind of love. That love, he says, "beareth all things, believeth all things, hopeth all things, endureth all things." And I see how puny what I called my love has been. Oh, it felt strong enough when Pauli was a baby and not touched by worldly sin. Now he's a man—a human, sinful man that offends my notion of what I want him to be. I remember last night and the

naked lady, and my charity's weak, and I want to cut him
out like a carbuncle and cast him away from me. Just the
way I did Frederick years and years back when I let Karl
have him to raise. Sometimes I wish I'd grabbed that little
red squealing animal out of the warming oven and run
outdoors and dropped it down the outhouse hole—directly
through the doorway to Hell.

Stop that. Saint Paul says that's not what love's about.

I'd give the rest of my days if I could set my Pauli
down and make him understand all of the truth he only
got a little bit of at the supper table tonight. Maybe then he
could be the son I always hoped he'd be. He's most likely
down at the trailer right this minute, having his own love
tested. To think your mother slept with a carnival freak is
bad enough, but to find out she did it with her own
brother. What man's charity is strong enough to bear that?
I want to explain how it was. I sinned, yes, but not in the
ways he thinks.

All these years and I never once said I love you out
loud—not to Jake, not even to baby Pauli. It seemed too
powerful, like magic words that could make things disap-
pear. I'm seventy years old. Time's ticking away. God help
me, I'm going down there tonight and speak my piece.
And after I tell Pauli how I got Frederick against my will
and after I tell him about Jake, maybe he can see my side
of it. I can forgive him if he can forgive me.

All of a sudden, I'm not tired anymore. I shut the
Bible and put the magnifying glass down on the table beside it. Lord knows I been quiet long enough. The silence
of lies has been broke. I broke it here tonight. There'll be
no more keeping still for me. I got the power of truth on
my side now, no matter what.

It's like it says in John 8:32, "And ye shall know the truth, and the truth shall make you free." Free! The very notion gets me to my feet.

While I'm getting a lantern down from the nail in the pantry to light me to the trailer—no more sneaking around in the dark for me—something that's been buzzing way in the back of my mind comes pushing forwards. Something Frederick said about papers to prove Karl's age. Didn't I keep all my old report cards from school in my bedroom chest of drawers? Maybe some of Karl's are in there too. Before I forget, I'm going to go look. It won't take but a minute.

I light the lantern and go into the front hall. There's no room for it in the pantry, so the old chest of drawers is still upstairs in the room that was mine when I was a girl. The door to the back stairs has been nailed shut ever since the tornado, but the wide front stairway is open, no way to close it off. I keep it swept and clear of cobwebs up to the first landing, but nobody's been beyond that in I don't know how long.

A good grip on the handrail and I test each step to see if it's still solid enough to hold me. I don't weigh much more now than I did when I was a youngster going up the back stairs every night to get undressed in the dark and crawl underneath the crazy quilt and into my bed. I just move a little slower these days, that's all.

Spiders have hung dusty curtains across the upstairs hall. On towards the front of the house, the floor slants down and away. Holding up the kerosene light, I can see the gaping black doorway to Karl's old room. Across from it, the door to Mutti and Vater's room leans open, and wild stalks of weeds and tendrils of trumpet vine poke through. I can hear the night crickets singing outdoors.

Good Lord, I wish I'd brought my broom with me. I wave my free hand ahead of the lantern to clear the darn cobwebs away. The dust itches my nose and makes my eyes water. In my old room, the lantern's flame reflects back from the three windows in the bay. The glass is grimy and cracked across a couple of panes.

I set the lantern down on the floor and tug open the dresser drawers one at a time. The veneer's curled loose, and the drawers scrape and stick. The top two are empty, but the bottom one holds Mutti's faded wedding ring quilt. I squat down and lift up its folds to see what else I saved under there. In one corner are a few of Pauli's baby clothes I brought up here and put away years back. Why? Whatever for? And next to the clothes is the hen toy I made for him. The print's gone gray, and the rag stuffing's come out through a ripped seam. I could mend it and wash it up. It'd be almost good as new.

What in the world am I thinking of?

Now, truly, it's not too late for a grandbaby. I'm commencing to warm to the notion.

Maybe when I tell Pauli the truth and he finds out his father's no freak, he'll decide he can find himself a girl and get married after all. He's half Jake. He could make fine youngsters. It's not too much to hope. Didn't Saint Paul say love hopeth all things?

But he didn't say love getteth all the things it hopeth for.

Underneath the baby clothes, my fingers touch something hard with a square corner—Miss Miriam Benson's *Jane Eyre*. I lift it out and turn the small brown book over and over in my hands. Just for a moment, I long to open the cover and read by lantern light just like I did when I was a girl. No time tonight. Maybe tomorrow or the next day. It comes to me—no need to hide it anymore. And I smile. I slip the book into my apron pocket and go back to looking for the report cards. But I stop. I recognize the sound of the pickup turning off the county road. A flash of headlights across the ceiling of the bay and it's racing up the drive. It doesn't slow down till too late. Metal crashes against concrete, and the truck engine dies. I panic and turn the lantern clear down, killing the flame.

Before I can figure out why I'm tingling, hand and foot, with fear, I'm over at the bay window. I wipe away the grime with the hem of my apron and look down at the pickup nosed into the back stoop. The headlights go out. The truck door swings open, and Frederick tumbles out into the bright moonlight. He disappears around the front. The back door bangs.

Like Lot's wife, I can't move. But my heart is racing in my chest, running away and going nowhere.

Downstairs in the kitchen—a gunshot!

"Gerta!" I say and clap my hands over my mouth.

The back door bangs open again, and Frederick comes out, waving the rifle and hollering, "Karl, you fucking bastard, where are you?"

From down by the outhouse, Little David is barking now, and soon his tail waves yellow white above the weeds. He's running towards Frederick, yipping and yapping. Frederick lifts the gun, takes aim, and fires twice. The barking stops.

"Karl!" Frederick shouts again. "Where the fuck are you?"

In the ice-white moonlight, he strides cross the ruts of the barnyard and down the smooth-walked path towards the outhouse. He grabs the door and yanks it open. It tilts back on one hinge. Inside, Karl's beard glows in shadow like a patch of snow. He's standing there, not moving, like he's already a dead man in a wooden box. I squeeze my eyes shut just before the shot sounds.

My old legs won't hold me up anymore. I fall down on my knees and drop my forehead onto the window sill. Down in the barnyard, Frederick's still cursing Karl. "Damn you. I hope you burn your fucking balls in hell, old man."

I lift my head and see Frederick's come back towards the house. He's wandering around in circles now. Every few seconds, he raises his head and shouts, "Hannah! Goddamn it, where are you?"

Something moves down by the windbreak, flashes in the corner of my eye, something light in the darkness. Pauli! No! Don't move, Pauli! Stay there, son, don't come any closer! I'm sending him messages the only way I can. If I try to shout a warning, Frederick's sure to catch sight of him. I watch horrified and pray—Please, God, please, dear God, don't let Frederick see him.

A flutter of wings in the moonlight and a barn owl flies up out of the tree Pauli's standing under, flies up towards the stars. I look back down at Frederick. He's stopped, still, drawn by the flare of white feathers. He points the gun.

I claw at the window, trying to raise it up, to yell at him, to make him stop, but it's nailed shut. Vater again!

I slide down to the dusty floor, moaning.

Oh, God. Oh, God. My poor Pauli, my baby, my love.

Chapter 22

1987

I want to raise my voice and cry out and beat my dried-up, old lady's breasts and tear my clothes and mourn in the ancient, biblical way. *Hannah!* he hollers through the rooms downstairs. I crouch on the slanty floor where I crawled deep into the tangled vines of Mutti and Vater's ruined bedroom. Woodbine and trumpet vine grow up around and cover and hide me. Heavy footsteps on the front stairs. *Hannah!* he yells from close by in the dark of the upstairs hall. The floor under me shakes with his heavy footsteps. Silent, I am weeping, the same as Rachel in the Bible, that wept for her babies and wouldn't be comforted. I am stuffing fistfuls of leaves—bitter and sharp—into my mouth, and sweet trumpet flowers. I am stuffing my mouth to keep myself from letting out a howl that'll give me away. *Hannah!* I shouldn't care to keep on going now my Pauli's gone. But I'm not ready to quit. Not yet. If my time is here, dear Lord, You'll show him the way.

Hannah! Fainter now, farther away. Dearest God, if You don't lead Frederick to me, I'll know it's You that's saved me. *Hannah!* Outdoors, from the other side of the house, I hear a gunshot fired into the air, and then another one. After that, silence. Even the crickets are scared to sing. Another shot and another one and the monster wails, *Hannah!* Again it's silence. Then, a cry. *Mother?* Oh, Frederick, I want to call out to you. Yes, I am your mother. And whatever love is, I loved you too. Curled here in the dark, I see my Pauli was just a pretty notion, like Jake was. Frederick, you are real, you are evil, you are my tormentor, and, flesh of my flesh, I love you just the same. I gave you your life. But you cannot have mine. Now the slam of metal and the snarl of the engine starting and the pickup backing and turning and speeding out the drive and away down the county road. Dear God in Heaven, the angel with the flaming sword that stands by the mailbox at the end of the drive and keeps me in, let it keep him out. I got to calm down. I got to think straight. Soon as my heart stops banging around in my head, I got to figure out what comes next. Frederick'll be back, looking for me. Daylight, he can see my footprints in the hallway dust. I got to hide where nobody'll find me, keep moving out of sight till Frederick gives up or the sheriff finds out and comes poking around. There's bound to be gawkers once the news gets out. But nobody's going to gawk at me. I'll just stay hid till folks give up and go away. I know lots of places—the hayloft, the cottonwood grove down by Turkey Creek, the rusting pickups and tractors out in the pasture—lots of places. They'll get tired of looking for me and figure I ran away someplace for good. I can outwait anybody. Things'll quiet down. There's plenty to eat in the cellar. *Jane Eyre* is in my pocket. I'll fetch my chickens indoors to live with me, put them in Karl's room. Folks'll drive by and point at the house. Nobody'll know I'm here. This is the home place, my place. Free of them all. I'll never leave it. I just got to make sure Frederick can't ever come after me again. Downstairs, I'm going to take Gerta's lipstick and write on the kitchen table oilcloth—FREDERICK DID IT. Oh, my Pauli. They made me out to be crazy, but I'm not. I did, I do, what I have to do to survive. Now I'm free. The truth has made me free, but my mouth is filled with bitterness. I keep on ripping the leaves off the vines and pushing them into my mouth to keep myself from crying out—my sons! my sons!—rising up and crying out in lamentation like the angels in Heaven in their white nightdresses and golden wings and halos like wedding rings, hovering over the suffering earth, tears running like rivers to the seas, weeping and mourning for us sinners, living and dead, all waiting and waiting till the end of God's time.

About the Author

P. B. PARRIS was born in a small Nebraska farm town. Daughter of a military officer, she grew up in the United States, Canada, and Europe. She attended the Writers' Workshop at the University of Iowa and completed a master's and a doctorate in English at Drake University. Ms. Parris presently teaches at the University of North Carolina at Asheville. She is the author of numerous short stories, one of which, "Little Orphan Betty," received a PEN Syndicated Fiction Project award in 1988. *Waltzing in the Attic* is Ms. Parris's first novel, and she is presently working on a second, set in New Orleans and Oxford, England.

The text of this book was set in the typeface Berkeley
Old Style Book by Berryville Graphics, Berryville,
Virginia

It was printed and bound by Berryville Graphics,
Berryville, Virginia

Designed by Anne Ling